Be

Not Afraid

Jeanne Chabot

PublishAmerica
Baltimore

PublishAmerica has allowed this work to remain exactly as the author intended, verbatim, without editorial input.

ISBN: 978-1-4489-2936-8
PUBLISHED BY PUBLISHAMERICA, LLLP
www.publishamerica.com
Baltimore

Printed in the United States of America

For my guardian angel whom I call Sam (which is short for some unpronounceable angel name)

Thank you to my husband Marc and to my children Alex, Dominic, Maryssa, Gabriel and Nicolas for putting up with late suppers and slightly chaotic schedules.

Thank you to my sister Rose Anne and to my friend Pascal for their encouragement.

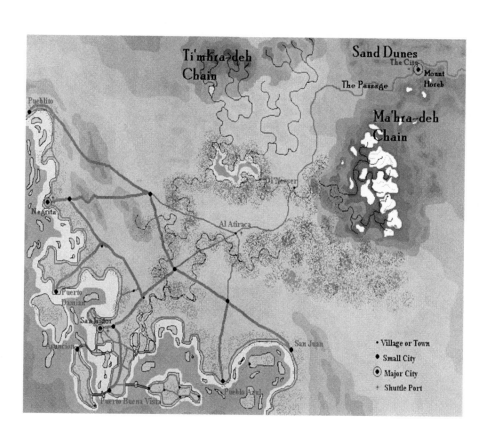

Ti'mh̄ɪa-deh
Chain

Sand Dunes
The City
Mount
Horeb

The Passage

Ma'hɪa-deh
Chain

Pueblito

Di'Nescen

Negrita

Al Atiraca

Puerto
Damian

San Isidor

San Juan

Junction

• Village or Town
♦ Small City
⊙ Major City
+ Shuttle Port

Puerto Buena Vista

Pueblo Azul

Book One

I

The terrace of my parents' house sits on the edge of a cliff. Some 50 metres below is a long stretch of sand running from east to west. Once, thousands of years ago, a large river probably ran through here, but it dried up long ago. At the edge of the cliff, the city stops. To the North, on the other side of the Passage, as we call the dried up riverbed, lie sand dunes. Every year, foolhardy people get lost in those inhospitable hills. To the south, on the other side of the city, lies the Ma'hra-deh mountain chain. The mountains stretch from East to West along the passage and from the terrace, they are visible, beyond the east end of the city, rising up dark and forbidding, they are just as dry as the hills to the north.

A steep staircase leads down to the passage from the terrace, as is the case with all the properties situated on the edge.

On that fateful day that was to be my wedding to Asur, the sun beat down on me as I stood at the edge of the terrace, looking down at the Passage. A delicate breeze lifted tendrils of hair around my face, but did little to cool me down. The Passage was particularly busy, with people rushing past on foot or passing by on the backs of camels. Everyone was in a hurry.

It seemed the whole world was running from something. I only wished to pick up my own skirts, kick off my shoes and run, to where I did not know.

I rested my elbows on the banister and laid my chin in my hand. I was desperate. There was no Prince Charming from ancient fairy tales in my story, ready to rescue me from what I thought was inevitable.

I had nothing against Asur, but I did not love him, nor did I want to marry him. I loved a young man from the working class, a mason by trade. My parents did not approve so our relationship was discouraged. We continued to meet whenever we could in small cafes in the working class neighbourhood.

I first met Ben Sha'rat when he was working on a new addition to my parents' already large house. At first, I did not pay attention to the quiet young man with dark wavy hair a little on the long side. One day, I came across him scolding a younger man. Neither of them noticed me as I observed them from the gate.

"I cannot have people working for me who steal." Ben said. He was holding a necklace that belonged to my mother. "I detest thievery. Besides, what kind of reputation would that give me?"

The younger man looked scared, "Please sir," he begged, "Do not tell anyone."

Ben looked at him a long moment. "Very well," he said. "But you must leave now. You will not come back to work for me and you will not expect to be paid for the work done here."

The other bobbed his head and headed toward the gate. I slipped into the shrubbery so he would not see me. As soon as he was gone, I came through the gate to the house. Ben was standing there waiting. I knew as soon as I looked into his eyes that he knew I had seen them.

"Here," he said, pressing the necklace into my hand, "I found this under the window. I believe it belongs to either you or your mother."

I stared into those dark serious eyes. "Thank you," I said, letting him know I would say nothing about the incident, "It is my mother's, I shall replace it right away." I turned to leave and he placed his hand on my arm. "Your parents will benefit from a small rebate," he said. "I have profited from an unexpected drop in expenses myself and would like to share the savings with your parents."

I nodded my understanding and left to put the necklace back in my mother's room.

It was not long after that Ben and two other men started putting the finishing touches on the walls. I came through the gate into the garden one day to find a row of exquisite blue tiles bordering the wall. I came closer to run my hands over the tiles. They were decorated with flowers and scrolls and motifs of all shades of blue on a white background. I was still admiring the tiles when I felt, rather than heard, someone come up behind me.

As I turned my head, a low voice murmured, "They are beautiful, are they not?"

I smiled at Ben. "Beautiful." I agreed.

"They were imported from San Isidor." He told me.

The next few days I took to watching the men work and Ben would stop every once in awhile and explain where certain things came from and the history behind different techniques. I knew he was attracted to me but he kept his distance. He knew my parents would not approve if he were to offer anything more than distant friendship.

****

I stood there on the terrace, in my white wedding gown looking down at the Passage, wishing I could disappear. I had stared at myself in the mirror just minutes before, barely recognizing the young woman in the reflection. My long dark hair had been pulled back gently in spite of my feeble protests. I had never rebelled against my parents before. I had never had a real reason to. I still did not quite believe that they would not consider my wishes to remain single.

The dress I was wearing had short sleeves made of very thin material because of the heat. I had no veil, but wore flowers in my hair instead. It was a simple but elegant dress, one I would have loved to be wearing in other circumstances, but today I hated it. I had walked out to the terrace behind the house to catch what little breeze was out there and to clear my head and think about what I was to do next.

Had I not been in love before, I may never have rebelled, but suddenly, like a geyser forcing its way to the surface, a strong sense of self-preservation, an inner desire to save myself rose within me.

I saw that I was alone on the terrace. Staring down at the busy passage below, I decided in desperation to try to escape down the narrow stairs. I had made it all the way down and had started to run a few steps when I heard a shout from above and then commotion. My parents are older now and my father no longer runs very fast. I knew I could outrun him and my mother and the female servants but my heart sank as I saw my cousin hurrying down the stairs after me. I dodged behind a camel and ran past a messenger going in the opposite direction.

I did not make it very far before Geoffrey caught up to me. He grabbed my arm and held on to me until my parents arrived.

"You dishonour me." My father panted upon his arrival. He was livid. "You will come back with us, you will stop making a fuss and you will marry Asur in the cathedral like a good girl!"

"I will not marry him." I told him calmly. In that instant, I could see clearly what I must do. "You can lead a camel to water, but you cannot force him to drink. You can lead me to the church, but you cannot force me to say 'I do.' I do not love Asur, and I will not marry him."

"It does not matter what you want." Hissed my father, "Your mother and I know what is best for you. With or without your active participation, you will marry Asur today." With that he turned on his heel and stalked back toward the house.

After that, they did not leave me alone. Within the hour, the Cathedral bells were ringing and a carriage pulled by white horses arrived at my parents' home to take the bridal party to the cathedral.

I entered the cathedral escorted by my father. Asur was already there, waiting at the altar, and the many guests were already standing in the pews. My father escorted me to the front with a grip so strong my arm hurt by the time we reached the altar.

The bishop and a young priest I did not know were there to greet us. The priest blessed us and mass started.

I did not listen to the bishop's homily. I paid no attention to the music nor the readings. When the time came to pronounce our vows, the priest invited us up to the altar again. I stood up and calmly took the three or four steps needed to reach the altar.

"Do you, Asur, promise to take Isabella as your wife, to love and cherish her, to protect her all the days of your life?"

"I do." Asur replied. I could not hold it against him. I knew that he honestly wanted to marry me. I knew too that he would keep his promise. I only wondered how he could stand there so calmly, surely knowing that I did not want him.

"Do you, Isabella, promise to take Asur as your husband, to love and cherish him, to support him all the days of your life?"

"No." I replied quite clearly.

The young priest looked quite taken aback. I could hear gasps from the front pews. Out of the corner of my eye, I saw Asur turn to look at me. I refused to look his way. I did not want to see the hurt that was surely evident in his face.

The priest turned to the bishop. "I cannot continue if that is the case."

My father rushed to the front. "You must continue," he whispered frantically, "She has had a bad day and is being contrary."

"But sir, I cannot marry someone against their will."

"It is her will, she will be grateful one day."

The Bishop intervened, telling the priest to continue.

The priest looked at him surprised. "But it will not be a true marriage in the eyes of God."

"In the eyes of everyone else, it will be." My father replied. "As for the eyes of God, we can deal with that later, re-marry them if needs be once she comes to her senses."

"Continue *Father* Bernadi." The bishop said firmly, reminding him at the same time of his position.

"I pronounce you husband and wife," he said against his will.

We returned to our seats.

After the final blessing, Father Bernadi turned to us and added, "Sometimes, in the life of a couple, one finds oneself in need of confession, especially in the first years which are a time of adjusting to one another." Looking right at me he continued, "If either one of you finds yourself in need of confession, please do not hesitate. I or another priest will be glad to help."

I understood at that moment that I had a friend, and more importantly, an ally.

****

"I am sorry that you do not care for me." Asur was pacing back and forth in the chamber that was to be our room from now on.

"I do not wish to be married to you, that does not mean I do not care for you." I tried to tell him. "We could have been good friends."

He was not really listening to me. "You do not care for me, but perhaps someday you will, if you give me a chance to show you..."

"I do not think anything will change." I told him. I entered the dressing room to undress for the night and closed the door. I came back out wearing a light nightgown and a silky robe. I had undone my hair and brushed it out. I began to remove cushions from the bed and arranged them on the floor in a corner of the room. Asur watched me uncomprehending. When I went to get a cover to lay over the cushions, he suddenly understood my intention to sleep alone.

"I will not have you sleeping on the floor," he said.

"I will not sleep with you this night nor any other night." I replied. "We are not truly wed, nor do I wish to be wed nor do I wish to partake in wedded activities."

"I will sleep on the floor then," he said firmly.

"If you wish..." I shrugged, not caring as long as I did not have to sleep with him and as long as he was not going to force himself upon me. I gave him a couple of pillows and watched as he arranged himself a sort of bed. When he went into the changing room to change into nightclothes, I crawled into the bed and lay facing the opposite side of the room.

After he had come back into the room and gone to bed and it had become apparent that he was not going to try to force me into anything, I started to relax. I knew he was not asleep, but I was sure he would not bother me. It had been a very trying day, I started to drift off to sleep.

I woke up in the middle of the night, startled, not sure what had awakened me. I realized from the breathing of Asur that he was awake. I did not know if he had slept at all. I turned over and tried to go back to sleep but the events of the day came to haunt me. I could not sleep any more.

How did I come to find myself married against my will to someone I did not love?

My parents are both from families of rich merchants, as are most of the people living in our neighbourhood. It has become common in the City, for marriages to be arranged among members of High Society.

People of high class in the City do not marry below their station. Arranged marriages were so common among my family and friends that I had never questioned them before, not until my own.

I wished with all my heart that it had been Ben who had been at the church to wed me. I remembered the way his eyes would light up when he talked about things that were important to him.

****

I had walked into a small pub with a friend one day not long after Ben and his workers had finished the new addition to my parents' house. It was not a pub that we usually frequented, it was not high class, but we were in the mood for a little drink and did not want to bother walking further. As my eyes became used to the dim light, I noticed several working class people sitting in chairs around a table in one corner. They stared at us, then turned their backs to us.

Alisha and I approached the bar and ordered two Altin Kurals, a mix of a malty-flavoured black tea called Assam tea and Ber Dew, a sweet alcoholic beverage made from bers, a type of fruit that grows well in our arid climate. When we turned to find a table, my eyes met those of a young man I had not seen when we arrived, sitting at a table on the opposite side of the room. It was Ben. He was with another young man.

I smiled at him and he got up to greet us. This earned us more stares from the group in the corner as it was obvious that we were not of the same class. I could see that Alisha was surprised to see me greet a working class man warmly, but I did not care. I was glad to see Ben again. He invited us to sit with him and the other young man whom he introduced as Karl Mboudo.

Karl had eyes that crinkled in the corners when he smiled as he was smiling then. "You are welcome to sit with us," he said, "but I fear Ben may bore you with his socialist ideas."

"I have never found him boring before..." I replied in a light tone. Ben gave me a look of appreciation.

"Ahhh, but he can be long-winded when it comes to certain subjects, and no offense, but isn't social justice and equality and worker's rights and such rather far from things you two usually ponder upon?"

I rose to the challenge. I was not going to be automatically placed in some pre-ordained class of people and dismissed so lightly. "Try me." I said.

"We were just talking about minimum salary." Ben said.

"But what is there to say about minimum salary?" I wondered, "Everyone has it, it's the law."

"It's the law, yes." Ben said gently, "But nonetheless, not everyone has it."

"How can that be?"

"Many people are paid under the table Isabella. The government knows this and yet it chooses to ignore it."

"But why?"

Ben sighed, and Karl grinned as he answered, "The government knows it will lose the support of big companies and business men if it decided to make sure minimum wages were respected. Big businesses like paying as little wages as possible and then selling the products at a high price. They make big profit. Why do you think your family is so rich Isabella?"

I was taken aback. I did not think my father was so dishonest as to refuse to pay minimum salary to all his workers. I was certain at least that those who worked in our home were paid at least minimum salary.

"Why would they take the job in the first place if they weren't getting at least minimum salary?" I asked, a little peeved.

Karl just shook his head.

"I don't believe you." Alisha came to my defense. "Isabella's father is not like that."

"Ask the people who work in his factories how much they get paid." Ben said. "I'm sorry Isabella, I know it is hard to believe, and you have never had much access to people not in your own class, but this is true. It happens all the time. It is why I started my own company, I wanted to have a just and honest company. I will likely never be rich or make huge profits, but what I make is enough and my conscience does not bother me."

"Some people have even made slaves out of workers." Karl went on to say. "They bring in desperately poor people from other places for a certain price, promising them a job, but when they get here, the company that hires them pays them practically nothing, their food and board is deducted, and the price they owe for being brought here and the interest on it is too high to pay off. They end up as slaves. They cannot leave until they pay, but they cannot pay with what they make."

I was aghast. I had thought that slavery was a thing of the past. I shook my head. It was too incredible. It was unbelievable.

****

I realized that I was shaking my head alone in the dark at the memory. I smiled at how innocent I had been. How injustices and slavery had seemed incredible in what I had believed to be an advanced and superior society. Since the day I had met up with Ben and Karl in the small café, I had begun to wonder about what they said. I actually went down to my father's factory one day in borrowed working class clothes, and got people to inadvertently tell me how much they were paid. Most were paid minimum wages, but many, especially immigrants or more desperately poor people who seemed to have no other choice, were paid under the table and their wages were cut in half.

I went to my father's friends' companies and found that everywhere, it was the same. The jobs no one wanted were given to desperate people who were paid very poorly for them.

Ben accompanied Alisha and I to her house the evening we had met in the café and then walked me home. We talked about different things along the way, his work, my family, art and culture, nothing heavy, but I was starting to have a lot of respect for this young man and I could sense something in him that I did not have but was starting to desire.

As we stood beside the gate to my home, I searched his face for some clue as to what it was that made him different from other people I knew.

He grinned as he said, "You are looking at me as though I am some alien and you have no idea what I am."

"I know *what* you are." I said, "I just don't know *who* you are. What is it you have that makes you different from others?

He laughed out loud. "How am I different from others?" he asked.

I tried to think, "You don't compromise." I said.

Ben raised his eyebrows.

I frowned, "No, that's not it." I said, "You don't...you don't compromise your values."

He nodded in understanding.

I continued, "There is something about you, I don't know, you seem content, and I think you wish this for others. You care for others in a way most people don't."

"Do you believe most people don't care for others?" he asked.

"Well, no." I replied, "But I think most people care for those they like, their friends, their family, and don't see beyond that. You seem to care for people in general, whether or not you know or like them."

We were silent for awhile. "It's not just that, there is something else, I don't know what it is. You seem more at peace than most people I know."

I was suddenly afraid of losing him, afraid that this would be the last time I would see him, afraid I would never know what gave him that peace, afraid I liked him too much.

I grabbed his hand. "I want to see you again." I said boldly.

He reached up with his other hand to briefly caress my cheek. "So do I," he said. I could feel my heart rate accelerate, I found myself wanting him to kiss me, but he dropped one hand and freed the other. "Tomorrow night I'll be giving a talk at the Red Camel Bar in the Id Safir Square. It starts an hour after sunset." He looked quickly at my clothes. "Find something less high class." He told me.

I looked down at the red dress I was wearing, with its full skirt, the details on the sleeves, and the lace at the throat. The medieval ages were almost a thousand years ago, and yet in many ways, although we are technologically more advanced, we in the City have gone back to those days. The automobile for example, is a thing of the past. The days in which women wore pants like men are long gone. The fashion has become for women to be distinctly women again, and so we either wear skirts or, for ease in work or play, tunics and leggings. High class women tend to wear skirts and dresses more often, while the working class women opt for the tunics and leggings for practical reasons.

Reluctantly (I thought) Ben started to back away. "I'll see you after the talk." He added and turned to leave. I watched him walk away until he turned a corner and I could no longer see him.

****

In the dark room, alone in the huge bed, a great sadness overcame me and despite the fact that I knew Asur was not sleeping and that he could likely hear me, I could not keep my tears away. I buried my face into my pillow and tried to think of something else.

I finally fell asleep again, and slept late. When I woke up, it was near midday and Asur was no longer in the bedchamber. I got up, stretched, and moved to one of the windows to look out. It was not the familiar mountains that usually greeted me from the window in my own room, with the city in the foreground. Instead, this window looked out over the Passage to the dunes beyond.

I could see part of the midday traffic below, many people on horses, camels or donkeys and many more walking or running.

My parents' house, in fact, our whole neighbourhood, is on a ridge. On the one side, the ridge ends in a steep cliff leading down to the passage. The most desirable homes in the city are built along this cliff.

On the other side, a more gentle slope leads down to the working class neighbourhoods. The households on this slope range in wealth, the wealthier ones are across the street from the houses built on the cliff, at the top of the slope, and as one descends into the city on any of the perpendicular streets, the wealth of the households also descends, until one reaches the working class neighbourhoods, also known as the Bowl. It is called the Bowl because it is a valley that is almost entirely enclosed.

To the south of the city, the Ma'hra-deh mountains border the Bowl. The ridge juts out from the largest of these mountains, Mount Horeb, and borders the bowl to the east and the north. Only to the west is there an opening to the Passage. It is also in this western end of the Bowl that most of the markets, trading posts and therefore many factories as well, are located.

Once, historians tell us, the Passage was a great river, and the Bowl was a large lake. Now, if it were not for several natural springs and many, many deep man-made wells, the City would be a very dry place. Trees do line the streets of the City, especially in the upper-class neighbourhoods, where there is more variety and many flowers, well watered by the wells. In the Bowl, except along the River Jordan and where it empties into A-S'Yloein Pool, one only sees the occasional fig or date tree and some others that do well in dryer areas.

The City would not exist in such an arid place except for the fact that it is halfway between the Seaport of San Isidor and the fertile continental lands surrounding the city of K'Raal. The City is a stopping place for travelers, a central location for trade between merchants from other cities. Because of its location, along the Passage, by far the easiest route from the continental cities to the seaside communities, the City has become a huge meeting place. There is always lots of action. The City used to be a town of Inns before merchants began to move there permanently to be closer to the huge markets. Now it is a bustling city with many permanent residents as well.

I decided to go down to the dining room to break my fast. The midday meal would surely be nearly ready and I was starving. I moved into the dressing room and changed into a simple dark blue dress and coiled my hair into a knot at the top of my head. I was ready to go down and eat.

I met my mother in the hall and she frowned at me.

"You are a married woman now Isabella." She said, "It is not seemly to go around as a maiden."

I had forgotten to attach a little piece of white lace to my hair. It was the symbol of a married lady of society. Well, I was not going to put one in my hair. I wanted neither to be married nor to be a lady of society.

"Mother," I said firmly, "Working class women have no distinctions between the married and unmarried. I do not intend, now or ever, to wear a little piece of lace in my hair for all to see and know that I am some high-class merchant's token wife to be dragged to society balls and brought forth as a decoration."

My mother looked extremely hurt. I was sorry as soon as I realized what I had said.

"Is that what I am to you Isabella?" she asked. "I used to be worth more in your eyes." She turned and started walking quickly towards her room.

I ran to catch her hand.

"I'm sorry mother," I pleaded, "I didn't mean it like that. I know you are worth more than that, I'm..." I did not know what I could say to explain how bitter I was feeling at the moment towards marriage. "You knew I did not want to marry Asur." I said finally, "I do not consider myself married at all."

I wanted to be more than just someone's wife, I wanted to share a purpose with him, a common goal. If only I could have been Ben's wife, it would have been enough, but I could not. I choked back tears. My mother could not understand. All she had ever wanted to be was the wife of someone who was her equal in society. I felt a need to go beyond that. I had a void to fill, something, I was not sure what, was calling me. And I could not have the man I wanted because the man I wanted was dead.

II

I left my mother in her room and continued downstairs. As I had expected, dinner was being prepared in the smaller informal dining room. Already, different plates had been laid out on the buffet to one side of the room. My father was sitting in a rocking chair in one corner, reading the newspaper. He glanced up to acknowledge my presence and continued reading.

Asur was standing, staring out the window into one of the gardens of my parents' home. My parents' estate is not huge, there is not a lot of land between houses in this very desirable area of the city, but there is enough land for the estate to have three small but distinct gardens plus the terrace in the back. This garden, surnamed the prickly garden by my father because my mother decided to have plants that grew well in the area and therefore had planted a number of different imported flowering cactuses and other prickly and thorny plants, as well as native plants. My mother called it the Rock Garden because in it rocks were strategically placed to set off different areas of the garden. The path through the garden was made from stepping stones, and a fountain in the middle of it all tumbled over small boulders. To the side of the fountain was a bench, made from a huge slab of rock laid across two flattened boulders. It was a very beautiful garden and I know my mother was quite proud of it. She had even done some of the planting herself, although she had left the heavy work to the gardener. Most women of her position would have told the gardener what they wanted and then left it to the gardener. My mother had to get involved. It was a way for her to express herself.

When I sat down at my usual place at the table, Asur turned and surprised me by sitting in front of me. It should not have been a surprise, but I had forgotten that everyone else considered us husband and wife. A married couple in high society always sat across from each other. An unmarried girl could sit across from another unmarried girl or a woman whose husband was not present. An unmarried man would likewise sit across from another unmarried man or a man whose wife was not present. I do not know how this custom started, but it did serve one purpose. At any formal dinner, one knew at a glance who was available and who was not.

My mother came in and my father moved to the table. My father said grace as one who had to do it, but would rather get it out of the way as soon as possible. He then turned to Asur and asked in a tone full of meaning if we had had a "good night."

"I slept very well last night," I said glaring at my father, before Asur could reply. "I can't answer for Asur though, since he slept on the floor."

"What!" my father roared. I continued to glare at him.

"I believe it is better not to push." Asur said hurriedly. "I must let Isabella get used to me. You would not have me force her!"

"No!" my father acquiesced, but he still was not happy.

My mother got up to serve my father and herself from the buffet. She signaled me to remind me that it was now my place to serve Asur. In high society, a woman always served her husband and any guests there might be, unless there were too many guests and the servants were asked to serve. It was a mark of respect towards one's husband and was reciprocated, as the job of serving the wine and any other alcoholic drinks came to the husband. If I had been willingly married I might have been proud to stand up and serve my husband for the very first time. As it was, I was beginning to be annoyed with what was beginning to seem like no end of customs designed only to remind me of my undesired situation.

I did not know what kinds of foods Asur liked so I put a little bit of everything on his plate. I noticed later that he seemed to be having a hard time swallowing down one particular dish that had cheese, mushrooms and spinach in it. I made a mental note not to serve it to him the next time.

My mother made a valiant effort to keep conversation going and Asur did his best to help. My father kept making innuendos about going to bed, which kept me glaring at him and even my mother was starting to get exasperated. I only spoke when asked a direct question and kept my answers short.

At one point she looked at both Asur and I and asked us what we planned to do that afternoon.

"I for one am going out." I said.

"Out?!" My mother's voice went up slightly in pitch. "Alone? But you've just been married!"

"You are married and that doesn't stop you from going out alone." I replied. I could hardly believe that this was me talking. It would seem that being married had had at least one effect upon me. I was becoming decidedly outspoken where I had usually always been rather quiet and obedient towards my parents before.

"But you were just married yesterday! People who have just been married don't want to be alone, they want to be with their spouse!"

I stood up. "I think we have all forgotten here that I didn't want to be married, that I said no to the vows yesterday, that in fact, one cannot truly say that we are married." My voice too had climbed in pitch. "I am going out, alone, whether you like it or not."

I glanced at Asur who was looking down at his hands playing nervously with his napkin. "I need to be alone right now." I said in a more gentle voice. "I will go out later with Asur."

I left the dining room and walked back up to the chamber I now shared with Asur. In the dressing room, I quickly changed into a long dark blue tunic and loose leggings, working class clothes. I slipped quietly out the side door and took the path to the gate, which went past the new addition that Ben had worked on for my parents. Flowers were now planted in blue and white flower boxes that accentuated the tiles I had thought so lovely when I first saw them.

I turned east on Paradise Lane and then south on Garden Street. I walked down Garden street to the working class area, then turned west on Stella Maris Avenue. I was headed for a little pub just off of Stella Maris Avenue, on Cardinal Road. It was the Red Cactus Pub. I had learned that most Pubs, when the name was the Red Something were gathering places for socialists and their friends. I happened to know that even at this rather early hour, there would likely be a small group gathered in the Red Cactus to exchange ideas, make plans or just be together.

As I walked into the Red Cactus and my eyes started to adjust to the dimmer light, I looked around to see if anyone I knew was there. In the far corner, away from the better lighted area that hosted a couple of dart games, was a group of young adults talking quietly around a table upon which a large candle was burning. The candle was there more for the ambiance than for the light, as there were dimly lit lamps to each side. I moved toward them and then one of them looked up and noticed me. The others glanced around to see what he was looking at and they all stopped talking at once and stared at me.

Karl was the first to move. He stood up, but he was on the other side of the table, the people on the near side came to greet me first.

"Bella! I'm so glad to see you!" One of the young women, named Fatima greeted me with a hug and an understanding look. Others crowded around, murmuring greetings. Karl waited until most people had said hello. He then grasped me by the arms.

I looked into his dark brown eyes which mirrored my sadness. We had not seen each other since we had laid Ben in the ground three months before. "How are you Isabella?" he asked. I knew he wanted a real answer.

"Let's sit down first." I said.

We moved back to the table and Karl pulled up a chair for me to sit beside him. When we were all seated, Karl said, "I'm glad you came back. For awhile, I thought you might not."

"You are my friends too." I replied, "You did not stop being my friends because Ben died. Your cause has not stopped being my cause because Ben died." I looked around the table at their faces. Fatima was to the right, on the other side of Karl, her dark features betrayed her Arabic origins. She was even darker than I and her hair was thick and long and straight. She worked hard to promote justice and had started a solidarity group among her co-workers. They worked in a carpet making industry, in poor conditions, little light, long hours and not much time for meals. They were not paid very well either, with the owners of the industry making huge profits. These were not ordinary rugs but beautiful hand-made works of art that were sold for much money.

Fatima was thinking of starting a co-op with her group of women, where each woman would invest into the company, and each would make the same profit from the sales. It was still only an idea, but she was starting to put it down on paper, and the rest of the group had given her possible solutions to different problems. Ben had contributed a lot to her idea before his death.

Beside Fatima was her husband, Alex who made quite a contrast in colouring. He was dark blond, tall and had blue eyes. Alex had worked with Ben in his company and had probably taken over since.

At the end of the table, beside Alex, was a stranger of medium height with the brown hair and brown eyes and medium colouring that are so common in the City. For centuries the City has been a mix of cultures. The Blacks, Caucasians, Asians, Arabs, etc, that have been meeting at this central point for ages and that have been living together for centuries have intermixed so much that they have created a new race. There are no longer very many true Blacks or Asians and someone like Alex, with blond hair and blue eyes, is very rare. Most people in the city have hair ranging from light to dark brown hair and brown or hazel eyes. This is one characteristic unrestricted by class. High society, as well as the working class, is mixed.

A girl I was familiar with but whose name eluded me was to the right of the stranger. She too had brown hair and brown eyes, but her hair was darker than the stranger's and it was quite wavy. It was just past shoulder length and she had tied a scarf over it.

Across the table from Karl and Fatima, quite literally filling up his chair, was Emile, a man in his thirties, with light brown hair and hazel eyes. He was quite overweight, but still attractive, with his jovial smile and his hearty laugh which always made people smile even when they did not know what the joke was about. I liked Emile and enjoyed his sense of humour. He knew how to laugh with people, even knew how to get them laughing at themselves when things went wrong, but was always very respectful towards others.

A much thinner man was sitting across from me beside Emile. He wore round glasses and seemed to fade into the background. This was an illusion, because usually when Ismael had listened to everything everyone else had said, he would suddenly lean forward and bring all the different bits and pieces together in a comprehensive resume, adding on things he had observed himself. He was so good at this, that he inevitably ended up as secretary or some similar position at various more official meetings.

To my left, between Ismael and I was Emile's sister Dominique. She was younger than Emile by about five years and thinner, but had the same light brown hair and hazel eyes. Her hair was long though and she kept it in a single braid down her back. She had an easy smile and was quick to laugh, but was more quiet than Emile. Dominique was the peacemaker. More than once, when arguments got heated, Dominique somehow managed to get between and say just the right thing to calm things down.

Karl signaled the barman over and ordered a mug of ale for me. When it came, he insisted on paying for it. Then he turned to me and asked, "So, what have you been doing in the last three months?"

"Do you remember I mentioned my parents had someone they were trying to interest me in so I would come to my senses and forget Ben?"

Karl nodded. I glanced around the table at the faces looking expectantly at me.

"They married me off to him!" This was said with a sudden break in my voice. I sounded half strangled. There was stunned silence. Apparently no one had expected this.

"What?!" Karl could hardly believe his ears.

"That's incredible!"

"You had no say in it?"

"They forced you to marry against your will?"

"I don't believe it!"

"What kind of parents do you have?"

I sat there barely hearing them. I felt Karl put his arm around my shoulders. "Enough!!" He said loudly. "Do you want to talk about it?" he asked me more gently.

"I just wanted you all to know." I said, "I thought you should hear it from me. They took me to the Cathedral yesterday and the Bishop and some priest were there and even though I said no, they still said we were man and wife."

No one spoke.

"It is not uncommon for the high class to have arranged marriages." I told them. "Most of the time though, both parties, although they may not be in love, are at least consenting, and most of the time the marriages seem to work out just fine."

I remembered something. "Wait," I said sitting up straight. "The priest didn't want to continue when I said no to the vows. He said it wouldn't be a true marriage in God's eyes if I had said no. The Bishop made him continue. He said something after, about how sometimes, especially at the beginning of a marriage, people might need to confess often…He offered to listen. He might want to help."

"You said no to the vows?" Karl laughed out loud. "Good for you!"

"Maybe the priest could do something for you." Dominique suggested.

"Maybe." I said.

"It's worth a try." Karl said.

"My father must have promised that Bishop lots of money for his church." I muttered.

"You should make an appointment to see that priest." Karl told me. "As soon as possible. Do you know his name?"

"The Bishop mentioned it, when he was ordering him to continue on," I said trying to remember. "Bernadi, Father Bernadi, that's it. That's his name."

"Go see him tomorrow." Karl said, "Before he forgets you, and before anything else happens to you."

****

It was nearing suppertime when I finally returned home again. I slipped in the same way I had slipped out, but met up with Asur in the bedchambre. I had hoped he would be out so I could change before seeing him again.

"You've been in the Bowl." Asur observed.

"It won't be the last time." I answered back. I instantly regretted my tone of voice. "Sorry," I said, "That was unnecessarily rude."

"It doesn't matter." Asur said.

"Yes it does." I said. "There was no reason to be rude."

I went into the dressing room and put on the same dark blue dress I had put on earlier. I re-arranged my hair in a knot on my head and purposely left off the piece of lace that was lying on the dresser.

"If you don't mind Asur, I would rather not eat with my parents again today. Perhaps you would like to take a walk and then find some café to eat in?"

Asur's face broke into a huge grin. "I must say, I was not looking forward to a repeat of dinner," he said.

I smiled. We were in agreement on at least one thing.

I went to find my mother while Asur entered the dressing room to change into something more suitable for walking.

I found my mother on the terrace having tea with my aunt who lives with her husband a fifteen minute walk to the west, almost at the end of Paradise Lane. They do not live right on the edge of the cliff as my parents do, instead their house is on the other side of the street.

"Good evening Auntie." I said, remembering my manners, "Good evening Mother."

My aunt Isobel, who happens to be my godmother, smiled at me and patted the chair beside her. My parents named me for her, although they changed the name to Isabella to avoid confusion.

"I regret I cannot sit down now." I said. "I came to let you know that Asur and I will be eating out."

"Would you let Filonia know please." My mother asked.

Filonia is our cook. She is not much older than me and has already been cooking for us for almost ten years. She started when she was sixteen. She is a very good cook, as was her mother. Her mother was the cook for my family before Filonia. It was when she became too ill to work that Filonia started to take on more of the work and eventually took over.

I went down to the kitchen where Filonia's younger sister Tessie was reading her lessons aloud. Filonia had not finished school although she

31

had come reasonably close before having to take over for her mother. She was determined that Tessie should get all the education she could.

"Hello," I said. "I won't be eating in this evening Filonia, and neither will Asur."

She nodded.

"Have you finished reading that book I lent you?" I asked.

Filonia's eyes lit up. "Not yet," She said, "but soon. That is a wonderful book."

I had lent her a book that Ben had given me. It was written in simple language and was full of everyday examples of the lives of ordinary working class people. It talked of better ways to organize society and gave concrete examples of ways different people had used to make their lives better. It was the first book Ben had given me and it was a turning point in my life. I was compelled to work towards creating a better society for everyone. It was not going to happen overnight, but I thought change could eventually happen.

"We'll talk about it later then." I said.

I stepped out onto the front porch to wait for Asur. He was not long in coming. He had changed into informal pants and wore a lightweight shirt. He offered me his arm and I took it as we walked together toward the street.

We avoided talking about our situation at all, and once we both relaxed, we actually had a fairly good time. I had always enjoyed Asur's discreet humour. He was quiet and did not seek attention, but he could make observations about things that were both true and humorous. We ate supper in a quiet pub that was middle class. The service was good, but the atmosphere was more relaxed, not as formal as a high class restaurant.

It was on the way home that Asur brought up the subject that we were both avoiding.

"I believe we should talk about our sleeping arrangements," he said. "I'm not sure that I will want to sleep on the floor indefinitely."

"Don't worry about it," I replied, "I can still go and sleep in my own room. I prefer my own room anyway."

"I see." Asur said, somewhat disappointed.

"My parents do not have to know." I added. "Not right away, anyway."

"I had hoped you might give me a chance." Asur told me. "Do you think you might be able to love me if you tried?"

I looked down at the street beneath my feet. "I don't know Asur, I don't think so. I think we could have been good friends, I don't think I could be more than that."

"We could give it some time," he said.

"We could, but I don't think that would change anything."

I did not want to talk more. We continued on in silence.

****

The next day, near mid-morning, I left the house to go to the cathedral in hopes of finding Father Bernadi and going to confession.

I asked the housekeeper at the residence if a Father Bernadi was staying there.

"Actually, yes. Hasn't been here long in fact. Couple o' weeks at most. Could I ask who's callin'?"

"Oh, I just wondered about confession." I said, not wanting to say more. "I wondered if he would hear my confession."

"Well, he's not in right now, but someone else is available, unless you really want him?"

"I would prefer Father Bernadi." I said, could you tell him Isabella Campanare asked to have confession? I will come back later if you know when he'll be in."

"He should be back for lunch." The woman replied, "Always eats here."

"Thank you."

I turned to go back down the stairs and saw the very person I was looking for coming up the street.

"Isabella!" He greeted me warmly, taking both my hands in his briefly. I was quite surprised that he remembered my name.

"I have come for confession." I said.

"Of course." He replied, "Please come in."

The housekeeper was still standing in the doorway and Father Bernadi squeezed past her ample figure with a muttered "Excuse me." I followed him and felt the woman staring at me as I passed. I decided that I did not especially trust the woman.

Father Bernadi showed me to what was his office.

"Please sit," he said indicating a chair at the far end of the room.

"For propriety's sake, we shall leave the door open, but also because people have less tendency to listen at doors they cannot hide behind."

I nodded.

"We are far enough away from the door, that if you speak quietly enough, only I will be able to understand you."

He took a chair close to mine. He sat facing the door, not looking at me, but in such a way that gave the impression that he was ready to listen. I took it as a signal to start.

"In the name of the Father, and of the Son, and of the Holy Ghost, Amen." I began. "Bless me Father, I have sinned."

I hesitated. "I have been impatient and unkind, I have neglected prayer."

I looked down at my hands. "I am sorry for these and other sins, but I would also like to talk about my marriage."

Father Bernadi turned to look at me then. "Yes," he said. "First, I absolve you from your sins." He gave me a short penance to fulfill. "Now, tell me about your marriage."

"Father, I never wanted to marry Asur. I wanted to marry another man who is now dead." Tears threatened for a moment and I held them back.

"My parents did not want me to marry the man I loved. He was working class. He had his own company. He worked on an addition to my parents' home. That is how we met."

"We started talking about things, when I got to know him, I started to respect him. He was a very good person. He had socialist ideas. He wanted a more just world and was determined to live his life in a just way. He started his company because he didn't want to work for an unjust employer who would take advantage of him and because he wanted to offer the opportunity to others to work for a just employer. He didn't compromise who he was. He had high standards for himself and he wouldn't back down, you know what I mean? I really liked that about him. He had something else too. I think he had a really strong faith in God and in the goodness of humankind."

I paused. "Before I met him, I think you could call my faith mediocre, but I guess you could say that he woke something up within me. I found myself going to mass sometimes even on weekdays. We prayed together sometimes. I think he prayed a lot. I found myself getting very involved in social action."

"Father, I do not see the goodness in human kind as he did. Not anymore anyway."

"Something has happened to make you doubt the goodness of humankind." He observed, inviting me to continue.

"This man, his name was Ben, was killed because he believed in the goodness of humankind." I said bitterly.

"I am sorry." There was nothing else he could say.

"We were at a fairly large gathering. Ben was already recognized as a persuasive speaker with intelligent ideas."

"Ben?" Father Bernadi suddenly interrupted me, "You are not talking about Ben Sha'rat are you?"

"Yes." I replied rather surprised. "Did you know him?"

"No I did not, but I think I would have liked to have known him. I heard him speak once. He was a powerful speaker. So you were his soul mate." He mused.

"I was his lady friend. We were secretly engaged. My parents opposed our relationship and we thought it best not to tell them yet. Only a few close friends knew about our engagement. I think my parents would have tried to forbid me to see him sooner or later but they were hoping that Ben and social justice was just a phase I was going through and that I would eventually come to my senses. If we had told them that we were planning on being wed, I don't know what they might have done to separate us. I don't think they realized how serious we were."

"I see." Father Bernadi paused for a moment. "What happened at this gathering?"

"Ben was one of the people who was going to speak. I was even going to go up after him and add a few paragraphs. It would have been my first time." I said sadly.

"Ben left to drink some water at a fountain before speaking. There weren't many people around. It was the perfect opportunity…" I choked on my words. I could not continue. Tears ran down my cheeks. I covered my mouth with my hand, trying to get some control.

"Let it out." Father Bernadi advised. "It is okay to cry. It will help."

I nodded, still not able to speak. Father Bernadi handed me a tissue. I blew my nose and gained control of myself.

"Someone walked by and shot him with a pistol." I said. "I thought those things weren't around anymore."

"A lot of things that aren't supposed to be around anymore still are."

"In the confusion, the person got away. No one knew who he was nor why he had shot Ben. The only description we could get was of a man in his late twenties to early thirties, of average height, short brown hair and brown eyes and a moustache. That could be almost anyone here in the city."

"I heard the shot, but didn't know what it was. I saw that people were running towards where Ben had gone to get a drink and suddenly I had a horrible presentment." Tears were falling again. I breathed in deeply to gain control.

"When I got to him, he was already dead." I sobbed.

Father Bernadi patted my shoulder. "That's it. Let it out." He encouraged me.

Someone must have heard me crying after a few minutes and come to the door, because I heard someone speak softly to Father Bernadi.

"Well, you know how it is when you come to confess to Father Bernardi." He replied jovially, "Either I make them feel incredibly guilty, or else the relief from the burden of sin is overwhelming!"

I could not help myself, in the middle of a sob, I giggled. I heard a soft laugh from the doorway and looked up to see a young nun standing there. Father Bernardi was grinning and winked at me.

"I will not bother you anymore. I just wanted to be certain everything was alright." The nun told me in her soft voice.

"It is." I replied, "I am feeling much better now, thank you."

The nun left the doorway and I could hear her footsteps down the hall.

"Thank you." I said to Father Bernadi. "I have not been able to talk about this to anyone since it happened."

"That's what I'm here for."

"Anyway," I continued, "The peacekeepers are certain that Ben was shot for his social views. Ben was making the people realize things didn't have to be the way they were. Ben and other people were showing them options to injustice, like co-ops, solidarity, working together, making our voices heard, educating ourselves. Ben's company was an example some other companies didn't like. Apparently, a sniper was hired by certain companies to get rid of Ben. All the peacekeepers have is hearsay. They have no proof. They can do nothing. All Ben ever wanted was to help people. They killed him for it."

"Leaving family and close friends to mourn his unjust death." Father Bernadi finished for me. I nodded.

"I know of a man who lived a long time ago." Father Bernadi told me. "He was a tradesman. Like your Ben. But he loved people. He wanted to help them. He saw an unjust society, a society blind to its failings, blind to sin, much like our own society. So he left his work and started to talk to the people about building the kingdom of God. He had friends who followed him and helped him in this new work, but none were as powerful a speaker as he. None have equaled him since."

"Men in power who did not like what he was saying got together to plan a way to get rid of him. They decided to have him killed. They had him falsely accused of a crime and put to death."

"On a cross." I said suddenly understanding.

Father Bernadi nodded. "And his friends were left in despair, suffering the loss of their beloved master who had been everything to them. They had thought him to be the Messiah, the one who would save Israel. So their faith was shaken too."

"Then God showed us how amazing He is. He used the worst possible scenario, the death of the Messiah to show us that he is even more powerful. Jesus was resurrected. Death did not win. In fact, Jesus's death was a sacrifice to save us from sin and not only that, but the conclusion of a new alliance between God and all nations. Through his resurrection, the story of Jesus, his actions, his words, his teachings became even more powerful."

"In the late twentieth century, an archbishop named Oscar Romero lived in a small country named El Salvador. He became very active in social justice. He was a leader and defender of the people. Those in powerful positions did not like what he was saying and doing. He was killed in the middle of saying mass one day, shot through the heart, much like Ben. But death did not win. In death, Monsignor Romero became a symbol of solidarity and justice. His words, his actions were remembered, were made public, books were written about him and the situation of the people of El Salvador. For years, people marched in different parts of the world, on the anniversary of his death to bring awareness of the injustices suffered by many."

"Some people have an expression," Father Bernadi continued, "In every cloud, there is a silver lining. I truly believe that in every despairing moment, there is the possibility, if you let him, for God to prove once again that he is still more powerful. Sometimes you only have to look, sometimes it takes time, but I believe that even out of something horrible, good can still come."

"I must thank you Father Bernadi." I said, "It has helped so much to talk with someone, and you have said,…some things,…that…things that help to make sense of it all. Things that encourage me to go on."

"I am glad to have been able to help somewhat." He replied. "I think your story is not quite over. If I have understood well, you have been married against your will?"

I nodded. "My parents, you remember, did not think seriously of my relationship with Ben. When he died, except to go to the funeral, I holed up in my room. I barely ate for days, and when I did, I didn't eat with them. I couldn't talk to them about it, they wouldn't understand and I didn't feel like going out and finding Ben's friends."

"My parents decided I was exaggerating and they were going to shake me out of it. They decided that the best way to do that would be to find someone else who would make me forget him. They knew that Asur was

38

very fond of me. They thought he would be perfect for making me forget Ben."

"I like Asur, he could have been a good friend." I continued. "But I do not love him. Not like I loved Ben. He keeps saying I should give him a chance, that I might learn to love him. I really don't think so."

"But why did they force you to marry him?" Father Bernadi wondered.

"They know Asur loves me. I think they were afraid I might fall in love with another working class man. They wanted to prevent that. They also really think that I could learn to love Asur."

Father Bernadi lowered his voice almost to a whisper. "You know that if you are married against your will, you are not truly married? A priest does not marry a man and woman, the man and the woman marry each other, promising love and fidelity to each other. A priest only blesses the marriage. You did not promise anything to Asur, I was told to bless your union anyway, but that still does not make it a marriage."

He had a sudden thought, "He has not, uh, forced himself upon you has he?"

"No." I said. "Asur is, if anything, very patient. He is capable of waiting, and I do not think he could actually force himself upon someone. But he can be very persistent sometimes. I do not know how long he will wait patiently."

"With my testimony of your refusal to marry Asur," he continued again in a very low voice, "It would be easy to get an annulment. The Bishop would not like that of course, because his judgment would come into question. It could have consequences for him."

"You could do that for me?" I asked. There was hope after all.

"I could, but it could take some time." He studied me a moment. "We must not say anything of this to anyone. I will write a letter and you must do the same, explaining your situation. While we are waiting, do not let on about anything. It might just make matters worse."

"I won't." I said.

I stood up and Father Bernadi stood up as well. "I thank you again." I said. "For everything."

"It is my pleasure," he said at the same time his stomach rumbled. I realized it was past noon and we had not eaten yet. "And it will also be a pleasure to eat soon," he said as we both laughed.

He showed me to the door, and I walked down the steps with a lighter heart and a lighter step than when I had arrived.

III

"Going to confession seems to have helped you quite a bit." My mother observed. I looked up. We were sitting in a small parlour whose large doors led out to the terrace. I was curled up in a huge stuffed chair, reading a book, while my mother worked on some craft. Asur and my father had just gotten up to walk outside a few minutes before.

"I haven't seen you this relaxed for some time," she said.

"Well you know how liberating it can be to be rid of one's sins." I said brightly. She studied me. I was not fooling her.

"You must have had a good talk with the priest," she said.

"I did." I replied, not offering any more information.

"I am glad it helped." My mother said softly. "I miss the old Isabella who was always smiling and passionate and happy."

I might have told her that it was hard to be happy and smiling when one's parents were forcing one to do something that was against one's will, but I decided to say nothing.

"I realize that you were not happy about being married to Asur." My mother continued. "I hope that you realize how good he is, how much he loves you. You could be really happy with him if you tried."

"Yes, Mother." I said returning to my book. I hoped she was done, I did not know how long I could dispassionately listen to her.

My mother lowered her voice. "Your father was not my first choice either," she said.

I looked up again in surprise. This I did not know.

"There was someone else. He was an artist. His father did not like his choice of career. He thought his son should do something that would bring in money if he wanted to have a wife and children someday. But I understood about his art. I knew how important it was to him. I have always loved art myself."

"Why didn't you marry him instead?"

"He left to study art against his father's wishes. I was introduced to your father. We were encouraged to wed, and so we did. It was the best choice of course. But the point is, I grew to love your father. We have been happy together. You can be happy too."

****

The next day, I delivered my letter to Father Bernadi, telling of the circumstances of my wedding to Asur. As I left the Cathedral, I was surprised to see Asur waiting for me.

"Been to confession again?" he asked suspiciously.

"You followed me here?" I asked.

"I saw you in the street and was going to catch up with you, but you turned in here."

"I was just leaving Father Bernadi something." I said.

"What?" He fell into step with me as I headed home.

"A paper,…" I said, "…on justice…social justice." It wasn't exactly a lie, as I did believe my marriage unjust. "Nothing that would interest you."

He turned to look at me then with hurt on his face. "How do you know?" he asked.

"Why would it interest you?" I asked.

"Why should it interest you?" He replied, irritated. "Do you think that you are the only rich person who could be interested in social justice? That you are so special? That the rest of us could never imagine enterprise without exploitation?" He snorted. "I have some things to do. I'll see you later." Surprised, I watched him stalk off.

****

Over the next few days, I began to get a feeling that someone was constantly watching me. I would look around or glance over my shoulder, but saw no one I knew, nor anyone who looked suspicious. I shrugged it off as my imagination.

Karl, Alex, Fatima, Ismael and the stranger that had been with the group at the Red Camel Pub were busy organizing a meeting. Since Ben had been shot, things had cooled down quite a bit and no one had organized any large rallies. There had been many smaller meetings between different groups of people however and this meeting would be the largest since Ben was killed. The stranger, as it turned out, was a leader of the group called Popular Action. His name was Sasha. Popular Action was a lobbying group for the rights of workers. They were also there to provide information to workers about their rights, about how the laws worked, and things they could do to try to ensure their rights were respected.

"People are afraid to come to these meetings." Karl was saying. "They are afraid someone else will get killed."

"I am afraid one of us will get killed." Fatima said.

"Father Bernardi told me something interesting." I told them. "He said that a long time ago, an archbishop who worked for social justice was killed. It only served to make his cause stronger, death did not win. People around the world marched on the anniversary of his death for years after that asking for solidarity and justice."

"I think you are talking about Monsignor Romero." Karl said.

"Yes, that's the one." I replied.

"You are right." Fatima said. "Death must not win. We cannot let Ben's dying be in vain. We must go on. They cannot kill us all, who would work for them then?"

"You were going to speak that last meeting, after Ben spoke." Ismael turned to me. "Would you like to speak again Bella? I think people need to know that there are upper class people who are willing to change things. It is not something we see very often."

I hesitated. "I don't know,…I have never spoken to a group before, and the last time I was only going to say a few things, sort of as a conclusion to what Ben would say…"

"It doesn't have to be long." Karl said. "Just tell them who you are, and what you believe. I think Ismael is right. It might be very good for people to know that some people in the upper classes have heard their cries and are on their side."

"I have heard stories of the son of a factory owner making changes in his factory." Sasha said. "Apparently, working conditions are much better since the son has been managing the factory. Everyone gets breaks, and they are longer. The son has had things like toilets repaired and has been renovating as much as he can to make the place more comfortable for those who work there. From what I hear, the father is still in charge, the son is only starting to take over. The people who work there are hoping that things will get even better once the son has taken over."

"Do you know who this person is?" I asked, very interested.

"No, it was all hearsay." Sasha replied, "You know, my cousin heard it from his sister-in-law, who heard it from her friend, who heard it from his brother…"

"So it might not even be true then." I said.

"It could be true." Sasha said. "I have heard the rumour a couple of times now, so there might be some truth. I'll let you know if I find out. On the other hand it could also be the product of wishful thinking."

"Things will never get better for people in general however, until the government makes new and better laws and starts enforcing them." Karl said.

"Agreed." Sasha replied.

"So will you talk then, Bella?" Fatima asked, bringing us back to the subject at hand.

"Maybe something short." I said, then I laughed. "Just don't make me the focal point! You might find people staying away for fear of boredom!"

We got up to leave not long after, and as we left the pub, Karl fell into step with me.

"So, you did get a chance to talk to that priest." Karl said in a low voice once we had said goodbye to the others.

"Yes." I replied. "It was so good to talk to someone about what happened."

"Can he do anything for you?"

"He's going to ask for an annulment."

"That's good news."

"It is."

We walked along in silence for awhile, then I noticed Karl frowning.

"What's wrong?" I asked him.

"I think we're being followed," he said.

My eyes widened. "Really?" I asked. "It's not my imagination after all?"

That caused Karl to stop in his tracks. "What do you mean, 'not just your imagination after all'?" he asked.

"For the past couple of days, I've felt like someone was following me, but I never saw someone suspicious, I just felt like I was being watched."

"I'm walking you home." Karl said. "Don't go out anymore unless you're with someone."

"What?!"

"You heard me! I'm serious. Don't go out unless you're with someone. You could get hurt. Stick to public places. Don't go up any back alleys. Someone could want to harm you."

"Did you actually see someone following us?" I asked.

"I'm pretty sure I've been seeing the same man behind us since we left. He's never too close, but not too far, and I don't think it is coincidence anymore."

Karl glanced around inconspicuously. "I don't see him anymore." He looked at me. "But I'm still walking you home!"

"What did the man look like?" I wanted to know.

Karl looked sideways at me. "Like a man from the City." He replied with a touch of sarcasm.

"Brown hair, brown eyes, medium stature." I sighed.

"The brown hair I can account for. I wasn't close enough to verify the brown eyes." Karl laughed. "But he wasn't actually medium stature, I would say he's a little on the tall side, not extremely tall, but not medium stature."

Karl is quite tall, and quite muscular, which made me very glad that he was walking with me. Karl has some african traits, something in his face, although his skin is the same colour as most people from the city, speaks of Africa. His eyes are dark brown, and his hair is also dark and quite curly. Karl was Ben's closest friend. They knew each other in grade school.

When we arrived at the gate to my parents' house, Karl warned me again to be careful when going out. He left quickly. He did not feel comfortable in high class surroundings.

My mother met me at the door. "Who was that man?"

"His name is Karl."

"Why did he come home with you?"

"He only walked me home, Mother." I replied.

"Why did he walk you home? Don't you know people will talk? You have a new husband and yet you are seen all over, in the company of everyone except him!"

"Don't you think you are exaggerating a little?" I asked. "I went out for supper with Asur the other night. People surely saw us then."

"But you barely show any interest in him! It's not right. People will notice and they will talk."

"Let them talk. I refused to marry him remember? I didn't make any promises! He might have married me, but I didn't marry him!" I stalked past my mother. It was becoming unbearable to be at home. I was tired of the nagging and people telling me how things should be, and that I should be happy. I decided to lock myself in my old room as I had done before.

When I opened the door to my room, I noticed right away that something was wrong. My personal items on the top of the dresser had been exchanged for a bouquet of flowers and a basket of sweet smelling soap, bath salts and other items. I looked around in a panic. My pictures had been taken down from the walls and replaced by paintings. My bed had a new spread on it that matched with the cloth over the night table. New curtains hung at the windows. None of my things were in sight. I jerked open drawers and closet doors. They were empty. My brows came together in a huge frown. I whirled around to go confront my mother and nearly ran into Filonia, arms full of cushions that matched the new bedspread.

"I'm sorry about your room." Filonia said in a faltering voice, not daring to look at me. "They made me help your mother to clean it out. We put everything into your bridal chambre. I am sorry. That is where they say you are to sleep from now on."

"It's all right Filonia." I replied. "I can't be angry with you."

"I put away some of your things, but the rest I left for you to decide how you wanted it. They told me to lock this door after." She looked around and lowered her voice. "I made sure there were plenty of extra cushions in your room and pillows too, if you need a second bed." She whispered.

"Thank you Filonia." I said surprising her with a spontaneous kiss on the cheek.

I decided to go to the chambre instead of confronting my mother right away. My pictures had been hung on the wall, my personal items now graced the top of a bureau in this room. All my clothes had been brought into the changing room. My books had been placed in a bookcase. Other items were waiting on the desk in one corner to be put away. I sat down on the bed. There was not much left to be put away. The rest was mostly souvenirs and decorations and I did not feel much like decorating.

I was still sitting on the bed when Asur came in. He looked at me then went to sit on one of the armchairs in what one would call the sitting area of our chambre. The bedchambre was actually a suite. At one end was the huge four poster bed, with dressers and night tables on either side. There was a window on either side of the bed, just over the two night tables. These windows overlooked the terrace below.

In the middle of the bedchambre facing the door, a loveseat had been placed in front of another window, this one looking out over the Passage. Two armchairs were placed at angles on either side of the love seat. Asur was sitting in the chair closest to the bed and therefore also facing away from it. I could not see his face. A table was placed between the chairs and loveseat and a rug under it all set the perimeter. Behind the unoccupied armchair was the dressing room which was also where our clothes were put. In front of the dressing room was a small bathroom.

I was staring at the small rug at the foot of the bed, when a pair of feet came into vision. I looked up at Asur. He still had a book he had been reading in one hand. He looked tired.

"I am sorry about your bedroom," he said. "If it means anything to you, I had nothing to do with it. I do not believe there was any need to go so far."

"Thank you." I mumbled, looking down.

He sat down on the bed beside me.

"A room is a very personal thing," he began. "I can't give that back, but maybe we can find a solution that gives you a little more privacy when you need it."

"Like what?" I asked dejectedly.

"Like drawing a line across the room with chalk and I stay on my side only." Asur said with a grin.

Even I had to smile at that.

"Sometimes I need to be alone too." Asur said. The armchair over there works for me since it basically faces two walls. I feel like I'm alone even if I'm not because I can't see anybody. What if we found a couple of screens and closed off another part of the room for you?"

I smiled at Asur. "That is a good idea." I said. "I am sure my mother has screens she doesn't use anymore up in the attic."

I stood up and headed for the door. Asur followed me up the narrow stairs to the attic. I turned on a dim light and looked around. There were boxes and chests and old furniture in every corner. It was hard to walk around up there.

"A lot of this stuff could be given away to people who might need it." I remarked.

"Why don't you do it?" Asur asked.

I looked at him in surprise. "It is not mine to give away." I said.

"Talk to your mother then." Asur suggested.

"You think she would want to give it away?"

"I think it would be better to sell it cheap." Asur said.

"Why sell it?" I asked, "It's not like we need the money."

"Sell it cheap," Asur said, "and donate the money to a charity."

I started to get excited. "That way, they won't mind getting stuff from the rich." I said. "Because it's for a good cause."

"And because they've paid for it, it doesn't feel like they're receiving charity." Asur added.

"Exactly!" I looked around, "There are plenty of things here. I am sure my mother will be able to donate some of it, and others have lots of things they don't want or need anymore either. I'll have to talk to the others about this!"

"The others?" Asur asked.

"Karl and the group."

"Oh." He started to walk around boxes, lifting covers to see what was underneath, and looking around. "Let's find those screens you were talking about," he said.

"Oh, yes, right!"

One screen was behind some boxes and the other was in the very back. I looked at it.

"It's all ripped." I said, "It needs to be repaired. I'm not even sure it could be repaired."

"Well, we have this one for now." Asur replied. "It looks like it only needs a little dusting."

We carried the screen back down to the chambre and I left to find a pail of water, rags and some cleaning solution. I found some in the kitchen.

"Why do you need stuff for cleaning?" Filonia asked. "Did I miss a spot?"

"Oh, no Filonia. We just brought something down from the attic and I wanted to dust it. I'll do it myself."

I met my mother in the hallway. Just an hour earlier, I might have snapped at her, but now I was in too good of a mood. Instead, I ignored her.

Asur and I cleaned up the screen and then set it up so the bureau in the corner, where Filonia had left my odds and ends, was partly hidden. It would be my private space from now on. Suddenly, I felt like decorating, now that I had a private space to go to again.

"Could you tell Mother I won't be eating please?" I asked Asur.

He just looked at me, then with a stilted "OK" he left the chambre. I had the distinct feeling he was not too pleased about something. I shrugged it off.

****

I was feeling hungry two hours later when I had finished arranging my things the way I liked. I felt like I had my own private world in that little corner. I had arranged the screen so it hid the corner from view almost everywhere in the chambre. I had moved the bureau over slightly and in the space left behind had piled some cushions to sit or rest upon. I had then arranged my things and when I looked around I was quite pleased with the little nest I had created.

Hunger drove me downstairs. I was about to pass by the parlour which led out to the terrace when I heard my mother's voice. I stopped.

"...difficult for you. She can be very stubborn, but she is a good girl. When she comes to her senses..." Teacups rattled.

"I do not believe she has to come to her senses." I heard Asur say. "She is not crazy."

"No, not crazy." My mother agreed, "But very stubborn. I think she actually believed herself to be in love with that man who was shot. Imagine that! My daughter with a common worker! I don't mind her being friends with them, they are people too, after all, but a marriage? It would never work!"

"Well,..." Asur started to say something but my mother interrupted. "I think you should take her to your home, Asur. Let your mother take care of her. It might do her some good to be away from her friends. She might spend some more time with you. She might learn to love you then."

"I don't know..." Asur hesitated. "I wouldn't want to take her away from things she loves, I don't think that would make her love me more."

"That, at least, you understand." I thought. I had heard enough. I went back up the stairs very quietly so they would not know that I had been there listening. Then I came back down again, making enough noise to be sure that they heard me coming. As I passed by the parlour, they were both sipping their tea quietly as if they had not just been talking about me a minute before. I continued on down to the kitchen, pretending that I had not noticed them.

****

I sat up late that evening, preparing notes for what I would say at the rally which was in a week. When I finally decided to go to bed, I got up, grabbed a cover and lay down on the cushions in my corner to sleep.

When I awoke, Asur was already gone. It was late morning. The birds in the garden were no longer singing. I could hear the traffic in the passage below. I was hungry again and went down to the kitchen to see if Filonia had any leftovers.

"I am starving!" I declared to Filonia. She smiled. I poked around until I found some bread, jam, and leftover porridge.

"I finished that book you lent me." Filonia told me.

"Good." I said, "What did you think?"

"It got me thinking maybe someday I could have a catering service instead of working in someone else's kitchen. Then I could charge my own prices for the food I made. Only I don't see how I can do that now. I would need a big enough kitchen. And I still have Tessie to get through school, if I didn't make money at first, who would help her?"

"You could start small." I said, "Do only deserts. You could work here during the day, and in the evening make deserts and see if anyone wanted them." Then you could add things to the menu if it worked."

"I guess." Filonia said. "It would mean more work though."

"It would." I replied, "at least at first. You could start off with only a few cookies and send Tessie door to door with samples so people would know what you make."

"You are right," Filonia realized, "Tessie is old enough to help."

"And you make such good deserts that someone, somewhere, will want some, I am sure of it." I encouraged her.

"I think I'll try it."

****

I decided to go out for a walk before returning to the talk I was preparing. I knew Karl was worried about me, but I was sure that as long as I stayed close to home in the upper class sector and on busy streets, I should have no problem.

I passed large homes, profusely decorated. At the corner of Paradise Lane, which is the street that follows the ridge for kilometres, and Saint Cecilia avenue, I turned south, towards the bowl, but stopped a few blocks down at a small café for a light lunch. Paradise Lane is the street on which all upper class families either have their home, or wish they had their home. Saint Cecilia is one of the busier avenues that lead down to the bowl.

I decided to eat on the terrace. I was sipping a sweet wine made from prunes and waiting for my seafood salad when someone walked up to me. Looking up, I saw Asur standing there.

"If you're not meeting with anyone else," he said, "perhaps you would let me join you?"

"Sit down." I said, glad to have some company.

"So," I asked, "where were you this morning?"

"Down at the factory."

"I thought your father had given you three weeks leave for your honeymoon."

"Yes, well I'm not having much of a honeymoon am I?" he asked. "I am bored, and although I do like your parents Isabella, spending all my time with them or wandering around doing nothing is not the way I prefer to spend my time. Besides, there was something I wanted to check up on."

"I'm sorry." I said.

"Sorry I wanted to check up on something?"

"I'm sorry you aren't having a happy honeymoon. You deserve better. I just can't give you better. You should be married to someone else."

"I would rather not be married to anyone else," he said. "Most girls I know are beautiful containers with nothing inside."

"And I am not?"

The way he looked at me made me regret I had asked.

"Maybe someday I will be able to answer that question." Was all he said. He signaled the waiter and ordered what I was having.

Our salads arrived at the same time.

"This is what you were having?!" He exclaimed. "I won't survive on this! I'm starving!"

"That is what you get for leaping before you look." I replied. "Try it, it's good. You can order something else after."

****

The next couple of days, I was busy helping to organize the rally and preparing what I would say. I went to mass in the mornings which I found very calming. I was quite nervous about speaking at the rally, especially about a subject I seemed so far removed from.

My mother noticed how distracted I was, and at dinner the night before the rally, she remarked upon it.

"Whatever is going on Isabella?" My mother asked, "It's like you're not even here. You barely talk, you don't even hear us talking to you. I have to repeat everything twice. You're not off to another one of those rallies are you? Not after someone got killed that last time."

"It's only a small meeting." I said. "Which I've helped a little bit with."

"A little bit?" My mother replied, "You've hardly been home the last two days and when you are, you stay in your chambre."

"Oh don't worry," I said, "It'll be over tomorrow and everything will be back to normal."

One eyebrow went up at that, but my mother said nothing. I think she was actually pleased that I seemed to be getting along with Asur, although I did not see him much during the day, and she was relieved that I had not made a fuss over losing my room. Also, I had been feeling more alive the past few days, I had found a purpose again to keep me going. I felt happier than I had been for the last three months. I am sure my mother noticed the difference in me and was glad for it.

The next morning, I went to mass again, but this time I decided to go to a small chapel in the bowl. I wanted to be with the working class at this mass before the rally. I sat in one of the back pews and after saying a short prayer, I waited for mass to begin.

I looked up as the priest came in and noticed that it was Father Bernardi. I was glad to see him again and thought I would chat with him after mass.

We stood up to listen to the Gospel according to Saint Luke which seemed as if it were written for me:

Meanwhile, so many people were crowding together that they were trampling one another underfoot. He began to speak, first to his disciples, "Beware of the leaven— that is, the hypocrisy—of the Pharisees. There is nothing concealed that will not be revealed, nor secret that will not be known. Therefore whatever you have said in the darkness will be heard in the light, and what you have whispered behind closed doors will be proclaimed on the housetops. I tell you, my friends, do not be afraid of those who kill the body but after that can do no more. I shall show you whom to fear. Be afraid of the one who after killing has the power to cast into Gehenna; yes, I tell you, be afraid of that one. Are not five sparrows sold for two small coins? Yet not one of them has escaped the notice of God. Even the hairs of your head have all been counted. Do not be afraid. You are worth more than many sparrows. I tell you, everyone who acknowledges me before others the Son of Man will acknowledge before the angels of God. But whoever denies me before others will be denied before the angels of God. "Everyone who speaks a word against the Son of Man will be forgiven, but the one who blasphemes against the holy Spirit will not be forgiven. When they take you before synagogues and before rulers and authorities, do not worry about how or what your defense will be or about what you are to say. For the holy Spirit will teach you at that moment what you should say."

"Do not be afraid of those who kill the body but after that can do no more." Father Bernardi started his homily, "Be afraid of the one who after killing has the power to cast into Gehenna." He paused to let the words sink in. "We are called today to continue the work of Christ here on earth. We are called to acknowledge the Son of Man."

"How does one acknowledge the Son of Man? Perhaps we could start by asking how is the Son of Man denied? Three great idols exist in every society in different proportions. People neglect Christ and follow these three: Money, Power, Sex."

"In the quest for money, the basic rights of people are trampled upon. No longer are we a community who shares our resources. Instead, a few take control of the resources and manipulate the production and selling so that they are the only ones who are profiting. People become objects

to be used in the gain of more money. Human life becomes dispensable.
"

"The quest for power goes hand in hand with the quest for money. People become pawns to be pushed about at will. It makes us feel important."

"The emptiness we feel inside needs to be filled and so we turn to sex. Sex becomes separated from love and life. The more we search for the ultimate sexual pleasure the more empty we feel. It is a vicious circle, ending in more and more deviant behaviour."

"Jesus calls us to go against these trends, to acknowledge him and the truth he has given us. God fills our life with purpose. When we are fighting for truth and justice and peace and solidarity, our lives are full. We are called to work together as a community for the good of all. It is how we were created. This is our purpose in life. This is what makes us truly happy. If we are not working for the general good, then we are working against it. It is as simple as that."

"Jesus was put to death because of the truth. People in his society denied our true purpose. People in our society today still deny our true purpose. Lives have been lost. Lives will be lost. But these lives will never be lost in vain. Jesus rose from the dead. God has showed that he has power, even over death."

"We too, have power over death, if we believe. When someone dies a martyr for the truth, it has an impact. Instead of killing the truth, it makes the truth stronger. When a brother or a sister dies, their death is never in vain. Death only strengthens the resolve of an oppressed people. It has been proven again and again throughout history. Death is powerless against us. We live on in the hearts of those who remain."

There was silence in the chapel.

Father Bernardi continued with mass.

After mass, I waited until most of the people had left to walk up to Father Bernardi.

"It's like you wrote that homily for me." I told him.

"In a way, I did." He replied. "I wasn't actually expecting you to be here to listen to it, but I did some thinking about your friend Ben, and the cause he died for. I know a lot of the people here will be at that meeting tonight."

I spent a few more minutes talking and then left to prepare myself for the rally that evening.

****

I met up with the others about an hour before the rally was to begin. I had decided to wear an older dress that was quite simple but was still of the upper class. The material was of good quality, dark green with a barely visible leaf pattern. It hugged my chest slightly and then loosened out at the hips. There was no decoration, no puffs at the sleeves, only some dark green trim on the edges. It was a dress for wearing at home when one just wanted to be comfortable. It wasn't a dress that most women from the upper class would have worn outside, but it was still of an obviously better cut and material than most of what the working class would ever wear. I didn't want to stand out, but if I was going to represent the upper class, I thought it would be better not to dress like the working class. I put my hair in one braid down my back, in the fashion of many of the women present.

Karl was already in the centre of the square calling for silence. The square was designed so that sound would carry from the centre to the outer edges. It was not only a park or a meeting place, it was also an auditorium. In the centre stood a square stone stage, upon which Karl now stood. He started his welcoming speech amid much encouragement from people standing around. He then welcomed Sasha as the main speaker.

Sasha was to give a talk on his organization, and the services that were available to the people if they needed them. He also would talk about their rights and what they could do to ensure they were respected. Finally he was to mention the different causes that Popular Action was currently lobbying for, and what they could do to help.

While Sasha was talking, I nervously went over what I was going to say in my mind. I looked around me at the people listening to Sasha. There were probably at least 500 people in the square, most were young to middle-aged adults, but a lot of people had brought children with them and there were also some older people. I watched two boys of about 7 and 9 ducking around people and bushes in a game of tag.

My feet were starting to get sore from standing there without moving when Sasha concluded his talk. Next came a question and answer period and then it would be my turn.

I started to move towards the front. It was starting to get cooler as the breeze picked up and night came on. Here in the City, there are no real seasons. From about November to January it gets a little cooler, and there is a bit more rain than the rest of the year. We were now in the middle of October.

A lot of people had questions for Sasha. So many people were now pressing forward, that I had a hard time getting closer. Karl decided to intervene. I saw him catch Sasha's eye and hold up two fingers. Two more questions and then Karl would introduce me as the next speaker. Sasha told the crowd that he would answer two more questions and then he would be available after the rally to talk to anyone who wanted more information.

I moved forward again, trying to catch Karl's eye so that he would know where I was, but he did not turn his head my way.

Karl stepped onto the stage again.

"Thank you Sasha." He started. "I know many of you would like to ask questions and Sasha will be available afterwards, but first let's listen to a new voice." His eyes were now roving over the crowd, trying to pick me out in the twilight. "Her name is Isabella and she is not from the working class as we are." He paused. "She is from the upper class and she is here tonight to show you that even among the members of the upper class, you have some support." He was still looking for me, so finally I stuck my arm up and then he caught sight of me. "Ahh, here she is," he said looking in my direction. People finally started to move aside as I passed by. There was a lot of murmuring in the crowd and I heard one surprised lady exclaiming "Wasn't she Sha'rat's ladyfriend? I never thought she was *upper class!*"

I joined Karl on the stage. He was grinning and obviously enjoying the surprise of the people. "Good luck." He murmured before leaving the stage.

"Good evening." I said. "I'm not much of a speaker. Not like Sasha or Karl. And not like Ben Sha'rat. I don't even have much to say that is news to you." My voice trembled just a bit. I cleared my throat and went on. "We all just wanted you to know that you *are* being heard, even if it is only by a few.

"I have seen the work you do." I said with a little more force. "And you should know that if it were not for the work *you* do, *we* would not be rich. The upper class may have the resources to get things to market and good business sense, but we couldn't go far if there were nothing to sell! You do quality work and it is in demand. You do *not* have to accept bad working conditions! You can organize yourselves and refuse to work unless your conditions are better. But you have to do this *together*. Or you can start your own businesses. You are smart people too! You can get together and create co-ops. It is easier to have partners and share in the expenses than to start out alone and with few resources."

"We have all been created equal and we, the upper class need to remember this. The earth is not for an elite, but for *everyone*. We must learn once again the simple rule we teach our children and forget once we have grown up: When we *share*, everyone has something and everyone is happy. We are human, created in God's image. Human life comes before profit. *Happiness* comes before profit. God wants us to be happy. *All* of us. It is time to open our eyes to the suffering of others and to put the welfare of everyone before the profit of a few. We must also remember that there is a higher law than ours. We are not obliged to obey our employers when what they want us to do will hurt others. We can stand together and fight repression! This is our *right*! And our *duty*! Thank you."

There was a short burst of applause and then Karl came back up to the stage.

"Short and sweet," he said in a low voice, "that was well done."

I left the stage and walked back towards the spot where I had left the others in our group. Karl concluded the rally and then indicated that Sasha would meet with whoever wanted to ask him questions. The square started to clear of people. Karl came over to join us as we talked over the evening and waited for Sasha who seemed to be busy with about 30 different people. By now, my feet were really hurting. I found an empty bench nearby and sat on it.

"That man," Karl said suddenly, "He's the one who was following us the other day Bella."

"That man?" Sasha said, surprised, "He's the one I keep hearing people commenting on since we got here. Apparently he is that Merchant's son, learning to take over from his father, the one who did what he could to make working conditions better in the factory he is in charge of."

I got up to look in the direction they were looking.

"That man," I said incredulously," is my husband!"

There was a collective gasp from the group. They started asking questions, but I was not listening.

Asur was apparently in deep conversation with a very admiring middle-aged working-class woman. He glanced my way, saw that I was watching him, and said something to the woman. She grasped his hand then, and bobbed her head up and down as if she were extremely grateful for something, and left him. Asur immediately came to meet me. I was so surprised to see him there that I could think of nothing to say. Or rather, I could not decide which question I wanted to ask him first.

"Excellent speech," Asur commented, "Excellent, but dangerous. I'll have to watch you even more closely after this."

I was still gaping at him.

"So you *were* following us a week or two ago." Karl said.

"Wait a minute!" I sputtered. "You mean to say you've been *following* me around?" I could not believe it. Could I have no privacy?

Asur held up a hand. "Before you get mad," he said, "listen to me."

"Well, it had better be good." I retorted.

"I got wind three weeks ago from some of my father's employees, not the workers, but the accountant and some of the overseers, that Ben Sha'rat's fiancé might be next on the list. Apparently they wanted to get rid of anyone who was close to him. Of course none of *them* knew who this fiancé was. But that doesn't mean the hit men don't. And the rest of you would all be on the list too." He added, "So I would lie low awhile if I were you."

"Why didn't you *tell* me?" I was still mad. "Don't you think that is information I might have wanted to know?"

"Well, I didn't know for sure if it were true or just rumour and I didn't want to scare you for nothing. I thought I might watch you for a while and see if anyone suspicious were following you."

"Did you notice anyone suspicious?" Karl wanted to know.

"I didn't notice anything and I haven't heard anything since. But tonight's performance will have put ideas into people's heads. There weren't just working class people here Isabella." He looked at Karl. "You know that. That is why you and your friend were careful never to go too far in what you said."

Karl nodded.

"Then why did you let her go that far? She didn't say much, but it was too much."

"I didn't know what she was going to say." Karl defended himself.

"Wait a minute." I said. "What was wrong with what I said?

"Nothing," Asur said, "except that you explicitly told them that they had power over the upper class and told them that not only could they use it, they had a duty to do so...In some other places, that might not be so bad, but here in the City, there are a lot of unevolved people who like to profit from ignorant workers and they prefer for them to remain ignorant about their situation. There has been a lot of change recently and more and more workers are fighting for their rights. A certain group of elites is not very happy about this, because they stand to lose a *lot*. The government is this close to enforcing minimum salary, and they know it," he said, holding his index finger and thumb a couple of centimeters apart.

"I hadn't heard that." Karl said, "That *is* good news."

"It *is*, for us. But not for them!"

IV

I had asked my mother if she would mind donating some of the items in the attic to people who might need them. So one day in late October we spent an afternoon in the attic going over the different objects that were up there. Inspired by that, I also asked my aunt Isobel if she had anything she could add. I ended up spending the next afternoon in her attic. The problem was, we didn't have any place to store the things. It was my father, surprisingly, who came to the rescue. He had an old building in the bowl, not too far from his factory that he didn't use anymore. He told me we could have the front half if we wanted and use it to sell the objects from. He told me that since everyone else was giving to a cause that he might as well give up something too. I think he was *also* only too glad to see my mother finally getting rid of certain items.

That Saturday, Emile Dominique, Alex, Fatima, Karl, Asur and I moved all the items we had collected down to the shop. The men hauled the things with a wagon while the women placed them in the shop.

I noticed that Asur and Karl were getting along very well together. I had not realized that Asur knew so much about politics, the subject had never come up between us. No, that was not true. It had come up a couple of times I remembered, but I had changed the subject right away, automatically putting Asur into the typical upper class politics category. I had been so wrong. I was guilty of judging a book by its cover. No wonder Asur accused me of thinking I was the only upper class person who wanted social justice.

A few more people had donated articles from their attics and we were wondering why no one had ever come up with the idea of re-selling used items before. Some of the things were very nice and in excellent condition and someone would certainly find use for them. I noticed

Fatima eyeing some of the furniture. "Uh-oh," I said to Alex, "Watch your wallet!"

Alex just smiled.

"This was a great idea you had." Dominique exclaimed. I glanced at Asur.

"Actually," I said, "it wasn't my idea. It was Asur's."

"Oh! Well, great idea Asur."

I handed Karl a packet of papers I had worked on, announcing the second-hand items to be sold, all profits going to charity.

"He's not so bad." Karl murmured.

"Who?"

"Who d'ye think?" He lifted his brow at me.

"Oh," I said glancing at Asur who was on the other end of the room, helping Dominique stack up some books on a bookshelf.

"No," I agreed. "He's a very fine person."

"Just not your type."

"Not the person I would have chosen." I thought about it for a minute. "But you know what Karl? There isn't anyone I'd rather be married to against my will,...except maybe you." I grinned at him. "In other words, I might have had a rougher time with someone else."

"In other words, you would only marry me if forced to." Karl pretended to pout. I rolled my eyes at him.

****

We opened the shop for business the next Saturday, and I got Filonia to make some deserts and get Tessie to sell them at a table. They would keep the proceeds of those sales themselves of course. A couple of women came up and asked it they could come and sell some things at tables too, and that is how an impromptu market set itself up in our shop.

At the end of that first Saturday, when the last customers had paid for their items and left, the money had been counted and put away, I stood outside the door, waiting for Karl to close up, and leaned against the front wall of the shop. The rough brick poked my back in places, but I didn't mind. A slight breeze played between the buildings and lifted my hair. I closed my eyes briefly in satisfaction. It had been a good day.

Asur came to stand beside me, as Karl locked the front door.

"That was fun," he said. "So full of life, in a way that high class gatherings are not. More relaxed I think. They are more at ease to be who they really are, less concerned with image."

I pushed myself away from the wall to stare into his eyes. For the first time, I noticed that they were lighter than my own, golden really, almost honey-coloured. I wondered why I had never noticed those specks of gold before.

"Who are you really?" I asked him. "I feel like I have been missing out on something. There is more to you than I thought."

"I do not know whether to accept that as a compliment, or an insult." He replied. His mouth curled up in one corner in a half-smile.

Asur reached out to smooth back a strand of stray hair that the wind was tossing in my eyes. I shivered involuntarily. He withdrew his hand stiffly and turned away.

"I do not mind your touch." I said, surprised by my own candidness.

He looked back at me, eyebrows raised.

Karl came to say goodbye just then and we headed off for home. The subject did not come up again.

****

Christmas was nearing and already it had been almost three months since the wedding. Asur and I still slept separately. He usually went to his father's factory during the day. I usually stayed home with my mother or went out with friends. We got into a routine where we would wait for Asur to come home before eating supper. Then, quite often Asur and I would leave to go for a walk.

It was Friday and a week before Christmas. Asur and I were walking in a park in the middle part of the ridge. With the extra rain bit of rain, many of the bushes were now in full flower. Mothers were calling in their children to put them to bed. Some adolescents were kicking a ball around at one end of the park.

"Let's just sit here for a while." Asur suggested, indicating a bench to one side under a fairly large tree. There were only a few trees in the park, but they were well-tended and watered regularly. Bushes fared better on their own than trees.

We sat down in comfortable silence for awhile.

"I was thinking,..." Asur cleared his throat. "I would like to stay with my parents for a time at Christmas. I was wondering,...well,...if you would come?"

I did not answer right away.

"I would like to come with you,..." I began, "I just don't like the idea that it confirms even more the idea that we are a couple. Oh, what does it matter, anyway? No one else even gives it a second thought anymore."

Asur sighed and look away.

"Asur," I said softly. He turned to look at me and I noticed how sad he looked. "I really do want to go." I told him. "If only because you are my friend, and a very good friend at that, and I would really like to see your parents, and the truth is, if you went alone,..." I stopped, unsure that I should go on.

"If I went alone,...what?"

"I would actually miss you." I grinned at him, hoping he wouldn't take it too seriously.

"Isabella," he said, "I think we should get the marriage annulled."

I stared at him in surprise, then looked away quickly, hoping I did not look as guilty as I felt.

"Well?" he asked. "Is that what you want? Because I can't be married to someone who doesn't love me. I can't handle it anymore. I don't know what made me do it in the first place, except that your parents had me convinced that you might be interested but that you were still trying to get over Ben and it wouldn't be long before you did. I almost stopped the wedding ceremony and walked out of the church when you said "no" at the altar. I don't think I've ever felt so bad in all my life. Number one, you were rejecting me in front of everyone, and number two, I was participating in some kind of plot to force you into marriage. I wish I had never listened to your parents. Let's go to the priest then, to see about getting this marriage annulled."

He looked closely at me then, and I squirmed. "That's a good idea." I said, not meeting his eyes.

"Unless of course you've already gone and asked for an annulment."

"I'm sorry." I whispered, looking at my hands.

"I'm sorry too," he said bitterly. "Sorry that you trusted me so little that you couldn't even tell me that you were trying to get our marriage annulled. Did you think I would try to kidnap you or force you to stay with me?"

"I didn't know what to think." I said, nearly in tears. "We thought it would be best not to mention it to anyone."

"We?"

"The priest and I."

"And how long ago was this?"

"Only a few days after the wedding."

There was a long tense silence.

"Have you had any news?" he asked.

I shook my head.

"In light of these events, I think it would be better if I went to my parents' place alone."

"Asur," I took his hand, looked into his eyes and pleaded silently with him to understand. "Please don't go without me." For some reason I could not explain, it had become very important to me that I go with him, especially now that he was withdrawing the invitation. "You really do mean a lot to me, and I *would* miss you."

"Isabella, why do you have to make it so hard on me? No, if we are to separate, it would be best that we remain as unattached as possible. I can't bring you with me. I have to make this as easy as possible for me to do. Do you understand?"

I nodded unhappily.

"Let's go," he said, standing up. We walked back home in silence.

****

Asur told my parents that he would be gone for a few days visiting his parents. My parents were quite surprised that he was going alone, but he was adamant about it, and I would say nothing. He left the next morning, taking most of his belongings. I realized that he was already preparing to move out permanently.

I missed him at supper that evening, and I went out walking with Alisha, whom I had not seen in a long time. We went dancing and I tried to put Asur as far away from my mind as possible. I should have been happy that he wanted an annulment. I should have been relieved that he was away. But I could only think of how much I had hurt him and how I wished he would come back and we could be friends again.

I felt melancholy all that week. Nothing seemed to interest me. Even going to work in the shop did not quite lift my spirits. I was restless and bored. I tried to read a book, but could not concentrate. I went on long walks but could not get rid of the restlessness.

I received a call on my com system on Christmas Eve. As I flicked on the system which allows one to communicate with anyone else in the world or to download information from the web, I saw Asur's face on the screen.

"H!" I said, very happy to see him.

"Hello," he said. "Are you folks going to midnight mass at the Cathedral?" He wanted to know.

"Yes." I replied.

"Well, I convinced my parents to go there, so we'll see each other there."

"Did you want to meet us at the door?" I asked.

"Ok, about 10 minutes or so before mass starts if we want to find a decent place to sit."

"Good. I'll see you then."

"Bye."

I let my parents know Asur wanted to meet us there and went to the chambre that seemed so empty without Asur, to get ready for mass. I chose a white dress that had a collar similar to that of a jacket, only it was much more feminine than a jacket. It had lace gathered in the V at least six inches long. It was of a cool, breathable material and was woven with bits of silver thread here and there. It had pearl buttons and a bit of a flounce at the bottom. Filonia came in to help me with my hair. We added a small poinsettia on one side. I wondered what I would wear around my neck when my eye caught a small box on my dresser that had been gathering dust. It was a wedding present from Asur and I had never opened it, although I had guessed from the box that it might be jewelry of some sort. I had forgotten it there until now. I picked up the box and opened it to find a beautiful three-strand necklace of cultivated pearls.

"It's perfect." Breathed Filonia. "You have to wear it with your dress. It matches the buttons!"

I agreed and Filonia fastened it on at the back of my neck.

Asur was waiting with his parents at the door when we arrived. He offered me his arm and we led the others up a side aisle to a free pew. The men were all wearing shirts of very thin material with white lace neck-ties. The lace was very simple for the men, not feminine, and the ties were knotted in such a way that they hung gracefully down from the collars of their shirts. My father even had a touch of lace on his cuffs and his neck-tie matched it. They wore loose-fitting pants of a light but more solid material. It is always hot in the city, even in the wetter season, and the clothes we wear differ therefore from clothes worn by people coming from the coast or the continental regions. Men from the continent for instance, wear leather quite often, even if it is only a belt, and do not have lace neck-ties but use cloth instead.

My mother was wearing a cream dress that had elaborate layers of very light lace around the throat, arms and hem. Asur's mother had a deep rose-coloured dress with a scoop-neck and no sleeves. Lace hung in folds from the shoulders instead, of the same deep rose colour. Lace is a symbol of class. The higher up in class you are, the more time and money you have to spend on making or buying lace. The irony is, many lower class women make very beautiful and elaborate lace to sell, but do not get to wear any. A lot of the lace is just expensive enough to make that they cannot afford to keep much for themselves and must sell most or all of their better lace to higher class people keeping the lower quality for themselves.

Asur and I entered the pew first, then my parents followed and last came Asur's parents. I knelt down to pray before mass. Since it was Christmas and midnight mass, there would be very old Gregorian chants instead of the regular music. The choir had been practicing and now suddenly burst into song. They sang a couple of old hymns and then fell silent again. The Cathedral was packed and people were standing at the doors. Mass was about to begin.

Except for a few of the hymns, most of the chanting was done a capello. I love listening to the human voice sing in harmony. The base sets off the soprano and tenor melts into alto and all the pieces fit and are one. To my ears there is no musical instrument that matches that of the human voice. How lucky are we to be able to sing in such a way!

Beside me, I could hear Asur's beautiful baritone voice. It was yet another thing I had not known about him, the man could sing!

When it was time to wish each other peace and Blessed Christmas, I turned to Asur and grasped his hand. "Blessed Christmas." I said smiling, "And peace be with you."

"Blessed Christmas." He replied, then saw the necklace of pearls around my neck. "You put them on," he said. I just smiled. It was time to wish my parents and his parents a Blessed Christmas.

When mass was over, we stayed outside on the steps of the Cathedral, talking for awhile. I wondered what we were going to do, or more specifically, what Asur and I were going to do, since both families probably already had plans and we would not all stay together. I hoped that he was not planning on going his own way and leaving me to go mine.

Finally, Asur took me apart and asked me, "Do you think it would be okay if I joined you? My parents are going to bed. They won't be doing anything until tomorrow morning...unless you're all doing the same?"

"Not a problem." I replied. "My Aunt and her family are joining us too."

Christmas has always been a big thing at our house. My mother prepares a great dinner for after mass and does not leave any space undecorated. My father always makes new wine in November and at Christmas we take out the first bottle of the five year old wine. My father lets his wine age for five years before we touch it. Here in the city it is customary to light a huge white candle inside the main window on Christmas night to remind us of the Light of the World. I did that as soon as we got home. I also lit a large white candle in the centre of our advent wreath which was on the table. The advent wreath was made from twisted palm branches and four advent candles, 3 purple and one pink were placed in it, one each for the four Sundays of Advent before Christmas. Ours also had little bells in it, representing joy, silk flowers representing hope and a couple of fuzzy white sheep figurines representing the shepherds who first heard the Good News.

My mother had organized a dinner of ham and roast lamb. Filonia had been very busy doing all that was asked of her and Tessie had to help her out. My mother had replaced all the candles in all the chandeliers in the dining room and I lit them. There were 10 chandeliers on the walls, three on either side and two on each end, each one held three candles, for a total of 30 candles. On the table there were an additional two candle holders, each also holding three candles. When all the candles were lit, and the table prepared, the room looked magical.

Everyone went to their place at the table, Asur taking his place in front of me, as usual, although he looked at me funny when he did it as if to say he would not be sitting there many more times. My father said the Christmas blessing over everyone, then said grace and the men sat down while the women went to serve their husbands and themselves.

I took care to avoid mushrooms while preparing a plate for Asur and I was generous with the pickled carrots which I knew he liked.

"Thank you" he said, the tips of his fingers slid over mine as he took the plate. To my surprise, it sent something like a jolt up my spine. I prepared a plate for myself and sat down. The talk around the table was hearty and jovial and my father had my Aunt aching with laughter over his jokes.

For some reason the morosity of the last week had left me. I felt as jovial as the others around me seemed to be. I met Asur's golden eyes across the table and my heart beat faster with gladness. The whole spirit of Christmas seemed to have taken me. There could be no other explanation for the joy in my heart could there?

My cousin Alexa's two little boys had their own little table but kept running around ours and sitting on indulgent adults' laps. I had the smallest one, Fredrick, in my lap and was cuddling him and feeding him grapes when I noticed his eyes were drooping. I held him close to me and rocked him, humming a little tune until he fell asleep. I looked up to see Asur watching me with a very tender expression on his face. I smiled at him and kept humming.

Alexa laid Fredrick down in a quiet corner of the house and we moved to the formal parlour at the front of the house. Asur sat down beside me. "I wish I could have had a picture or a painting of you just now." He whispered in my ear, "You looked very much like Madonna and child."

His breath on my ear did something very strange to me. I could feel my heartrate quicken. The skin on the side of my neck prickled. I felt positively euphoric, and to my surprise, I found myself leaning into him, wanting him closer, wanting his lips closer. I wanted him to keep whispering things to me. Anything. So long as we were this close. I could not understand it. This was still Asur; the man I could not love, the man who could never be more than a friend to me.

****

I was happy to have Asur back, but it still seemed like something was missing. I stayed awake late that night, even though we had gone to bed late and I was tired, turning over and over in my bed.

I got up later than everyone else the next morning. In fact, it could almost no longer be called morning when I finally pulled myself out of bed. I did not bother to dress. I pulled on my housecoat and went downstairs in my bare feet. I was greeted by a hurricane.

"Sabella!" Fredrick rushed into my arms. "You wake now. Me open pwesents!" His older brother Simeon followed and exclaimed "Yay! Now we can open our presents!"

"You didn't have to wait for me!" I laughed.

"Yes we did!" Simeon said with a bit of a pout.

"Poor you!" I laughed, pulling on his jutted lower lip.

When the presents for the children were opened, the gift boxes and tissue paper put away, and the boys happily playing with their new toys on the floor, the adults exchanged gifts. These were typically small and not always individual. For example, my cousin Alexa offered a basket of goodies to my whole family. Aunt Isobel, being my godmother, gave me an individual gift, a book I had once mentioned to my mother that I would like to read. I gave my parents a framed ink and watercolour picture I had drawn of children playing in a sandbox in late afternoon in one of the City's parks. It was one of my better drawings and I thought it would please my parents to have something pretty made by their own daughter, so I had asked Alex if he could find a good frame for it, and he had found something that set it off perfectly.

"I have something for you too," I told Asur "but it's in the chambre. I'll go and get it."

"I'll be outside in your mother's 'prickly garden.'" Asur said.

I took a small package out of the top drawer of my dresser, came back downstairs and turned to go out to the rock garden.

Asur was sitting on the bench beside the fountain, apparently in deep thought since he was bent over, frowning at the ground and did not appear to hear me approaching.

He looked up as I came up beside him and his frown changed to a smile. I sat down beside him.

"It's not much," I said, "But I made it for you."

He took the offered package and pulled back the tissue paper. Inside was a lace neck-tie I had spent many hours on in the last couple of months. It was all silk, and I had managed to find a design I liked that had something that resembled peacocks around the edges. I knew Asur liked those birds. I had changed the design slightly to add leaves in between. The middle part was mostly solid with just a few peacock shapes to break it up.

Asur stroked it with his hands to feel the silkiness. "This is beautiful," he said. "You are good with your hands."

"Thank you."

"It is I who thanks you."

He put the neck-tie back into the tissue-paper and put it into his pocket.

"I am not good with my hands," he said, "and I do not have much to offer besides my friendship,…."

"That is good enough." I said.

"But I do have something I want to give you," he said. "I have been sitting here trying to decide whether or not I should give it to you."

"Oh?" I said in surprise, wondering what it could be.

"I don't have it here with me, it's at home." He half-smiled at me. "Will you come with me for dinner?" he asked.

"Of course." I was very curious.

We left as soon as I was dressed. Asur's parents live on the other side of the city, across the Bowl from us in one of the newer, less prestigious but just as rich sections of the City. To get there, one has to descend into the Bowl and then ascend the other side. Their neighbourhood is part way up a mountain. It would take much too long to get there on foot, so we took a carriage. Even so, an hour had passed before we pulled up at the gate. The houses in this area are bigger than those on the ridge. The rooms are larger, and the estates are bigger. But it lacks the view over the Passage and the history of families being long settled and therefore it has not the prestige of the Ridge.

Dinner was very good. Asur's parents were very relaxed and easy to talk to. I especially liked his mother. Sometime in the late afternoon, after a few glasses of wine in the shade of a small tree in the back garden, Asur decided it was time he should be bringing me back home. He went to his room and came back with an envelope.

"I'll give it to you later." He told me.

We said goodbye to his parents and walked towards one of the busier streets to catch a carriage to take us back to the ridge.

At the gate to my parent's estate, Asur told the driver to wait for him, and I realized that he intended to go back to his parents' place. I tried not to show that I was disappointed.

Asur held out the envelope. He looked embarrassed. "I wrote this a very long time ago," he said, "so have pity on a 12 year old boy, okay?"

I looked up at him, wondering what could possibly be in the envelope, but he said nothing more about it.

"Good bye." He cleared his throat.

"I'll call you." I said.

"Okay."

"'Bye!"

"Good bye."

I took the envelope to the chambre and sat on the bed. I examined the envelope as if that would tell me what was inside. I got up and locked the door to the chambre so that I could be alone with whatever was inside that envelope.

Inside the envelope was a note and a much older envelope. I read the note first:

I don't know yet if you will be reading this. If you are, then I imagine it will have been because something finally convinced me to give it to you. If it was a bad choice, I hope you will forgive me. I only wish to share with you something of myself. This is how one 12 year old boy felt for one 9 year old girl. I don't ask anything of you, I just want you to know how far back it goes for me, that I have always thought you special. If I cannot have your love, then I will be honoured by your friendship.

I reached slowly for the old envelope and opened it. I pulled out an equally old piece of paper and unfolded it. To the left of the page was a drawing of a girl wearing a red dress with lace around her neck. The arms were a little skinny and the hands were a little too big. The head was slightly larger than normal and the nose looked a little flat. The girl had long, long, black hair and was smiling a bright (very bright) smile. She had huge brown eyes, but no eyebrows. The artist obviously thought the girl was very pretty and had taken great pains in colouring the picture and adding details. There were even darker red flowers all over the dress and a bracelet around one wrist.

At the top of the page was a title written in large capital letters: *WHY I AM GOING TO MARRY ISABELLA WHEN I GROW UP*

"Well," I thought tenderly to myself, "You did succeed at that...sort of."

Underneath the title and along the right side of the page was written the reason why:

Isabella is a beautiful princess. She could kiss a frog and turn it into a prince. She is really nice and shared her cookie with me today. She never says bad things to me and she doesn't let anyone else say bad things either.

She's not like other girls who just want to wear nice dresses and be pretty. Isabella likes real things. She even played catch the wolf once. So I am going to marry her one day and be her prince because she's the only girl that isn't dumb.

I couldn't help it. I had to laugh, with delight of course.

V

When I came home from morning mass a couple of days later, I checked my messages in my com system and there was one from Father Bernadi, asking me to come to see him at St. Gabriel's Presbytery as soon as possible.

As soon as I had broken my fast, I called St. Gabriel's to see when Father Bernardi was available.

"I have something for you." He told me. "It just came yesterday."

My heart thumped a little harder. It must be the annulment!

"When can I come?" I asked.

"Now, if you like, I have nothing until a confession at 11:00. How soon can you be here?"

"It's what? A 20 minute walk from here?" I asked.

"Make it 25."

"Then I can be there probably for around 10:15." I said, looking at my watch. It was just after 9:30. I had a few things to do before leaving.

"Ok. See you then."

"Goodbye."

****

I rang the bell at St. Gabriel's and it was Father Bernardi who opened the door. He led me to his office, leaving the door wide open as before. He took a fairly large envelope out of his desk.

"This came for you," he said, smiling.

I took it and opened it. Inside was a short letter and two certificates of annulment.

"The other one is for Asur." Father Bernardi told me.

"He will not be happy." I said.

"Do you want me to come with you?" he asked me.

"No," I sighed, "I have to do it myself." I looked at the priest. "He already knows that we applied for an annulment." I said. "He brought it up himself, he offered to get an annulment. Then he guessed that I had already asked for one." I looked sadly at the piece of paper in front of me.

"He was hurt I take it." Father Bernardi said.

"He was. He said he couldn't believe I couldn't trust him." Tears burned behind my eyes, but I refused to cry.

"It's not pleasant is it, when you have to hurt someone else to do what is right."

I shook my head.

"Well, someday he *will* forgive you, and someday he may even thank you." Father Bernardi said.

"Oh, I think he's forgiven me, or anyway, he's accepted that our marriage will be annulled, but it's going to bring up the hurt again to see it written on paper." I said. "I couldn't have asked more from him. Another man might not have been so understanding. I was lucky in a way. I could almost tear up the certificates now and just let him have me."

"You care a great deal for him." Father Bernardi observed.

I nodded.

"Do you love him?"

"I-I don't know." I said "I don't think so, not enough to be married to him."

"Do you think you could love him enough someday?"

I looked a moment at him. "You, know," I said, "I think, if I were given the chance to get to know him better, knowing I could decide myself, I might eventually learn to love him. On the other hand, I could also very well realize that I was right all along and he *isn't* the one for me."

Then I would advise you not to tear up the certificate." Father Bernardi smiled. "Anyway, tearing them up would do you no good. The marriage has been effectively and officially annulled, whether you keep the certificates or not. I suggest you give Asur his copy, and then ask him if he would like to start over again from the beginning. As if this had never happened."

"Thank you. That is a good idea."

"I have heard many reports recently, of people getting together to fight abuse from the Upper Class." Father Bernardi mentioned.

"Yes," I said, I have seen things in the newspaper too."

"Apparently telling them that they had power over the Upper Class has had some effect."

"Asur thought that was dangerous for me to say." I said.

"It most likely was. You will not be well liked by some people. I imagine your father must be feeling pressure from some of his business friends to keep his daughter silent."

"He has not said anything to me." I replied. "What do you think an ideal society would be like, Father?"

"I am not sure what an ideal society would look like." Father Bernardi said. "I think resources would have to be made public and not private. And work would have to be shared and equally paid. It is in human nature to work. It is our purpose. If we have no work, we lose our meaning in life, our dignity. We were created to work. We need to have a purpose in life. Without purpose, man wanders, he becomes depressed. Work needs to be equally shared, and the benefits as well. It is difficult to imagine how to do something like this. I think it might be easier if the community were smaller. It is harder to cheat someone you know well or like well. The error is to try to be socially just without love, without God. Some still profit more than others. The people are still oppressed. Whatever the ideal, it needs God."

"I would like a community like that." I said.

"Aboriginal communities once worked like that. Everyone had to pull their weight but everyone also benefited. If one did not contribute, he was hindering the community as someone else would have to do the work for him. Having a common purpose makes a community strong. However the danger comes when people are not motivated to work, because they can get away with not working."

"There needs to be a balance." I agreed. "People need to reap the benefits in proportion to the amount of work they put in."

"Yes." Father Bernadi replied.

****

I took a carriage to the West End of the City, to the factory that Asur was now managing. It was on a fairly busy street that connected to the Main Road leading out of the City. I paid the driver and stepped down. Immediately I was hailed by many street vendors, all boasting of their wares. I smiled and refused politely.

I had never been here before. Hesitantly, I entered the building, and found myself in a short somber corridor. I noticed some workers repainting the walls a pretty cream colour with brick red and sable accents. At the end of the corridor was a door, which I opened.

I entered into the main part of the factory. Music was playing in the background and people were laughing and chatting to each other as they worked. The lighting wasn't very good in here either, but it was better than the corridor. A man saw me looking lost and asked me if I needed something.

"I am looking for Asur Midfallah." I said.

"Oh, I can take you to his office." The man said.

"Thank you."

Asur was sitting at his desk with the door open when the man knocked on the door. "Someone's here to see yah." The man said, and left.

Asur looked at me in surprise and then invited me to sit on one of the chairs. His office was small but at least it was well-lighted. It had also been recently painted in the same colours that were now going on the walls of the corridor. There was one painting on the wall behind his desk, of a pool, with trees around it and peacocks and peahens in a garden.

"I received something today." I began hesitantly.

"The annulment."

I opened the envelope I had brought with me and took out a copy of the certificate for Asur.

"This is your copy." I said.

"I see." He took the copy, glanced at it and put it away in his desk.

"I read what you gave me the other day." I told him. "I'm glad you gave it to me. It was funny and sweet and charming..."

Asur was silent.

"I would offer to rip up the certificates." I said, "Except that it wouldn't undo the annulment."

"Why would you do that?" Asur asked me.

"Because I really, really hate to hurt you." I said, "and because I think I'm going to miss you more than I thought I would."

"But you still don't love me."

"Asur, I can't say I love you, not now." I took a deep breath. "What I would like to do, is start over. If you wish. I feel like everything got done backwards. It isn't until just recently that I feel I have gotten to know you."

Asur sighed. His shoulders slumped. He looked positively dejected. "Do you know what it is like to hope for something, to begin to think that it will happen, to be glad inside when everything seems like it is going to happen only to find out it wasn't happening after all, and then to hope and hope and hope that things will get better only to end up having no hope anymore? I don't think I can handle any more hoping. I need to move on. Please don't make it anymore difficult than it has to be." He stood up and paced across his office.

"This is not the way it should have been." I said, frustrated. "If I had been allowed time after Ben's death, to get over him, if I hadn't been forced into marrying you, maybe our friendship would have developed into something else all by itself!"

"I'm sorry." Asur said.

I got up to face him.

"Can't we start over?" I asked him, "Can't we pretend that we were never married? Isn't that what an annulment says? It never happened. We just happened to be together a lot recently and now our friendship is taking a turn. Maybe it will become something else, maybe eventually we will be able to marry for real, maybe we won't...but at least we'll have given it a chance. A *real* chance."

"I just don't think I can handle more disappointment," he said shaking his head. He looked at me sadly. "I need time to think."

"Then *take* time to think." I said earnestly. I stood up on my toes, reached up with my hands and pulled down his head to gently plant a kiss on his forehead. I heard his sudden, soft intake of air. When I let go, his eyes were closed. He opened them again and seemed unable to speak.

****

When I told my parents that I had never been truly married and that the church had officially annulled the wedding, my mother sighed loudly, but my father got very angry. He went on and on about what others would think, and about my reputation and about how selfish and ungrateful I was, until even my mother had heard enough.

"Stop it Ivan, that's enough!" She said firmly.

"But can't you see woman!" He exclaimed, "What do you think they've been doing up there in that chambre for the last four months? No self-respecting man will want her after this! For all we know, she could even be pregnant!"

"Then I guess it's not a self-respecting man I'd want as a husband." I interrupted. "Father, I'd like you to stay out of my business from now on. I want you to know that I will *not* let things go so far the next time. In fact, I think maybe it would be better if I just moved out."

But where would you live?" My mother was aghast, "How would you support yourself? You're not pregnant are you?"

"Mother," I sighed, "Did you think I would share a bed with a man I did not marry? Asur and I have never shared a bed. Not *once*. There are enough cushions in that chambre for two extra sleeping places. I refused to partake in wedded activities, and Asur, unlike some people," I started pointedly at my father, "respected my wishes."

My mother looked so relieved, that, if the situation had been less serious, I might have laughed.

"But you're not seriously thinking of moving out?" She said hopefully.

"I only just really thought of it." I said. "I don't know why I didn't consider it before. I think it would be best."

"I will never pay for an extra apartment in the City when you have a place here, girl." My father declared.

"You would not need to. I am sure I could find work somewhere. If you won't hire me in one of your factories, perhaps Asur will. At least with Asur, I know I'd have minimum wage." My father winced at that.

"You'll be happy to know that all my employees will be benefiting from minimum wage as of next week," he said. "As of next month, the government will be enforcing minimum wage. Businesses that don't comply will be fined. They are hiring extra agents to act as enforcers as we speak. Why don't *you* go and apply?" He added sarcastically.

"Well, it's about time." I said. "Maybe I *will* go and apply!"

I did not eat supper with my parents. I ate something light in the kitchen with Filonia and Tessie.

"If you really want to move out, you'd be welcome to move in with us." Filonia said quietly. "It's not a fancy place, but it's clean and there's room since John moved out, and quite frankly," she said, lowering her voice even more, "We could use some help in paying the rent."

"I'd like that, I said. "I'll have to think about it. I don't want to move in without knowing first that I'll be able to help with the rent."

I excused myself early, as I had a bad headache, and went up to my chambre. I was so emotionally exhausted and physically drained that I fell asleep at once.

VI

I awoke to screams. I jumped out of bed, grabbed my housecoat and raced downstairs.

There was a big commotion in the front of the house, near the gate. Tessie was screaming over and over, my mother was unsuccessfully trying to calm her. My father and the gardener were standing over something, no someone on the ground. My heart in my throat, I raced towards them. My mother saw me coming and tried to stop me but I went around her. Filonia lay there, dried blood staining her clothes at her chest.

I felt like I was going to be sick. My stomach contracted. Neighbours, hearing Tessie's screams had come out to see what was the matter. I felt like my head was turning. I grabbed onto Tessie and hugged her tightly. Together, we made it to a nearby bench, where Tessie burst into sobs. I held her tightly and rocked her back and forth as my head stopped reeling and my stomach settled. Peacekeepers arrived. My mother came to sit with us, looking a little dazed. My Aunt Isobel arrived. She went to the house and came back with whiskey in small glasses for the four of us. Tessie made a face at the taste but we encouraged her to drink it. "It will relax you." Aunt Isobel told her.

A search of the grounds revealed a note in the mailbox. It simply said: *"Your daughter talked too much. Now she will talk no longer."*

It was apparent that the assassin had made a mistake. I had been his intended victim. My stomach started turning again and I rushed off to the nearest bathroom. Aunt Isobel followed me.

"Are you all right honey?" she asked.

I looked at her.

"I know, stupid question, how could you be all right?"

"I feel,…incredibly guilty to still be alive."

"Don't you *ever* feel guilty to be alive!" Aunt Isobel exclaimed. "I don't claim to be knowledgeable on God in his wisdom, but for some reason you were spared. So you just keep on living and you fulfill your purpose!"

Filonia's body was brought into the house. Her brother John was sent for. He came quickly with his wife.

"We will pay for funeral expenses." my mother told him. When he started to object, she said, "It is only right that we should honour her, who died in our daughter's stead." John accepted without another word.

Eventually, things started to settle down. John's wife took Tessie home with her, while John went back to his small shop. The police took the body with them, as they wanted an autopsy done, and the Cathedral was notified of the death and a time was arranged for the funeral. The place became silent again, but it was a sad and scary silence. One peacekeeper stayed at the gate to watch our house.

I realized it was almost 2:00 and I still had not had anything to eat. I did not feel like eating. I went up to my chambre and sat in the chair that Asur had often sat in to read the newspaper or a book. I stared out the window. Time passed.

I heard footsteps behind me. I did not turn around. Asur's arms went around me as he sat on the edge of the chair. My mother must have sent for him. Somehow she knew that even if we had gotten the wedding annulled, we still cared for each other. He half-lifted me into his lap while maneuvering himself into the chair. I buried my face in his shoulder and wept, while he rocked me, much as I had done with Tessie that morning.

I do not remember falling asleep, but I remember suddenly coming awake when Asur shifted his legs. For a very brief moment, I had a feeling of peace and security, like a child in her father's arms. I wanted to stay there. Then I remembered what had happened and who I was with.

I sat up quickly. "I'm sorry." I said.

"Don't be."

"You must be tired."

"I'll admit," he said with a wry smile, "You *were* starting to get a little heavy."

I stood up and so did he. "Come here" he said, leading me to the love seat, "This will be a little more comfortable."

We sat down side by side and he put his arms around me again.

"It's all my fault," I said sadly, "You were right, I should never have said what I did."

"It is not your fault." Asur said. "You did not pick up the knife to stab Filonia. The person who did is guilty of murder, not you. And maybe the person who paid him to do it too. You only told the truth."

"I still feel terrible."

"I know." Tears ran down my cheeks again. "You have to leave." Asur said "You can't stay here anymore. I'm taking you home with me. Our annulment has been made public, so hopefully no one will think you are with me. You cannot go to the funeral Isabella." He looked at me seriously. "Once the assassin realizes his mistake, he may well try again."

"I can't even go to the funeral?" I asked in a small voice.

Asur shook his head. "It's too dangerous." We sat awhile longer before he turned to me again.

"You will have to say goodbye to your family for awhile," he said. "You can't stay in the City any longer. We have to get you out."

I looked at him in shock. Not stay in the City any longer?

"You don't have to leave right away," he said. "You can stay with us for awhile. But you do have to leave soon. We'll have to make arrangements for you to go either east or west. You don't have to think about it now, I just wanted you to know that you will have to choose eventually where you want to go."

"I don't want to go anywhere." I was distraught.

He hugged me tight, "Think of it as an adventure." He murmured close to my forehead as I started to cry again.

After a few minutes I calmed down and Asur let go of me. "We have to get you packed now," he said. "Don't leave anything you will want later behind, but try to stick to essentials only." He went to the door and I noticed that there were a couple of suitcases there. I quickly went through my clothes and packed what was necessary. I threw in a few grooming accessories. I picked up the small box with the pearl necklace and placed it in one suitcase. I picked out a couple of books, and placed them in too. Then I took the envelope that Asur had given me at Christmas out of my desk.

"I am definitely taking this with me." I said.

****

"You have to help Tessie." I told my parents, "Filonia died because someone thought she was me. Now Tessie has no one to make sure she gets an education. If you don't help her, she will have to work too and she will never have a better life. Please help her."

My parents looked at each other. My father cleared his voice. "I am sorry I forced you to marry Asur." He told me, "I should have let you make your own choices. I was wrong. I will help Tessie, for you, and for Filonia. Filonia was a very good girl, and we will miss her."

A carriage had been sent for, and it pulled up in front of the house. Asur and I climbed inside. A peacekeeper accompanied us inside and another rode outside with the driver. I felt very sad to be leaving my parents and very frightened at the aspect of leaving the City behind. I was silent during the ride to Asur's parents' place.

Asur's mother greeted us at the gate to their property. Asur brought in my suitcases, and his mother showed me the room I would occupy. Asur insisted that I join them in the kitchen for a light supper. I had not eaten much all day and realized that I was hungry. I also had a very bad headache.

Asur's mother noticed I was rubbing my temples and my eyes and asked, "Is your head hurting you?" I nodded.

"Asur, would you go get my chamomile and lavender massage oil?" she asked. Turning to me she said, "Come lie down on the couch in our family room, I'll give you a head rub. Chamomile and Lavender are good for calming and relaxing you and the massage should help your headache."

"Oooooh," Asur said, "you will love my mother's head rubs, they can cure anything!" He winked at her and went off in search of the oil.

Asur's mother led me through double doors into a small, comfortable and informal parlour, their family room she called it. "Lie down here." She told me, indicating a long couch that was placed up against a window that looked out into their back garden. I lay down and when Asur came back with the oil, she sat down at my head and placed it in her lap. Dabbing oil on her fingertips, she proceeded to gently massage my temples, my brow, the ridge of my nose, behind my ears, the back of my neck and my crown. I closed my eyes and breathed in the scent of chamomile and lavender. I could feel the tension lifting, I no longer felt any pain.

When she was done, I sat up and my headache, as bad as it had been, was gone. "That is positively magic!" I exclaimed. "I have no more headache!"

"Didn't I tell you she could heal anything?" Asur replied. His mother just smiled.

"Thank you so much." I said.

"It is my pleasure."

After a bit of soup and some bread and cheese, I felt even better.

"You should get some sleep," Asur's mother told me, "You must be exhausted."

"I *am* tired," I said, covering a yawn with my hand. "Even though I *did* sleep a little bit earlier." I glanced wryly at Asur who smiled back at me. His mother caught the look but said nothing.

"I am going to go to bed as well." Asur said, standing up. We walked to our rooms together.

"Good night." Asur said.

"Good night."

Once alone, I found I could not sleep. I kept seeing Filonia lying on the ground with blood all over her. I kept wishing there was something I could have done. I wondered why I was still alive while she was dead. I wondered if Tessie and John would blame me for her death. Why did everyone around me have to die because of the truth? I cried myself to sleep.

****

I got up as soon as I started to hear other people moving around the house. I was not sure how this household functioned and I did not want to miss out on something important, like breakfast for instance. I dressed in a very simple burgundy dress, and clipped my hair back. I found my way back to the kitchen where the cook was already preparing breakfast. Asur's mother was with her, talking and even putting her hand to a spoon now and then, something my mother would not have done.

"Coffee?" asked Asur's mother holding up the pot.

"Oh, yes," I replied, "I will be needing some this morning!"

We sat together at the kitchen table, sipping our coffee.

"We usually eat breakfast in the small dining room out there." Asur's mother pointed in the opposite direction of the double doors leading to the family room. There was an archway, leading into a small corridor. Stretching out my neck, I could see there was another room just beyond. "Breakfast is served at 7:30, Asur and Abel usually leave around 8:30 for the factories."

Asur was already in the dining room when we entered. He had obviously come in through the other door, off the main hallway. He looked up and silently passed me part of the newspaper he had been reading.

There I was on the front page, in a picture taken at the wedding. The headline read: *ATTEMPT ON CAMPANARE HEIRESS'S LIFE: Servant is killed by mistake.* I started to read the article:

Just days after Isabella Campanare received a certificate announcing the annulment of her marriage to Asur Midfallah, an attempt on her life was made. The assassin made a mistake however and murdered a family servant, Filonia Connaught instead. The Campanare family is honouring Miss Connaught with a grand funeral to be held in the Cathedral this Saturday at 14:00. Miss Connaught's youngest sister, Tessara, has been taken in by Ivan Campanare and his wife.

"Isabella wanted us to take care of her, since Filonia was gone and could no longer pay for her education." Says Elizabeth Campanare. "In memory of Filonia, and because we will miss Isabella, we accepted. She will be like a daughter to us."

Isabella Campanare has left her parents' estate and, according to Mr. Campanare, if she has not already left the City, she will be leaving very soon. Her destination is a secret.

Miss Campanare was involved with socialists and social justice workers, and at one point was very close to the now deceased Ben Sha'rat. Ben Sha'rat was himself assassinated for his views on society. Miss Campanare assisted at a social justice rally last October, in which she was quoted as telling the people: "If it were not for you, we would not be rich."

Miss Campanare was closely connected to friends of Ben Sha'rat with whom she opened a shop, where they sell used items and donate the money to charity or social justice. This shop is located in one of Mr. Campanare's buildings. He assures us that the shop will remain open as long as Miss Campanare's friends want to take care of it.

Peacekeepers still do not know who the assassin might be, and are working on the case around the clock. It is suspected that the assassin was hired by someone else, and peacekeepers are looking for clues as to whom this person might be.

There was a smaller article describing Ben's work for social justice before his death, an even shorter one on Asur, and a second article on the second page about me, where I had gone to school, awards I had won, things I had done etc. I noticed that not much was said about Filonia. I passed the page on to Asur's mother and sat down at the table beside Asur. He took one of my hands and squeezed it.

"Well!" was all she said when she had finished.

Asur's father came in to join us for breakfast.

"Good morning." He smiled at me.

"Good morning."

"I see you are the latest volcano to explode." He remarked.

"Yes, I seem to be a *hot* topic." I replied.

"Ma, Pa," Asur said, "I think Isabella should stay here for awhile." He looked at me and continued, "The newspaper says that if she isn't gone already, she'll be leaving very soon. If the assassin is still trying to kill her, he'll be checking all the transportation out of the City. I don't think she should leave until at least a month. We have the peacekeeper here posing as a gardener, and anyway, most people won't suspect she's here, since our marriage has been annulled. They'll think we're feeling hostile to each other."

"And you're not?" His father teased, winking at me.

"Of course Isabella should stay." His mother said.

"It would mean staying here all the time though. You can't go out anywhere," he said, looking at me, "You'd be recognized and it would be too easy to find you again."

I sighed. "I know I'll find it hard," I said, "but I can do it,...if your parents can put up with me." I smiled at them.

"Of course we can." Asur's mother assured me.

"Then it's settled." Asur said. "If you need anything, just ask me and I'll get it for you." He told me.

****

The house seemed very empty with Asur and his father gone to work. By late afternoon, I was feeling quite restless. I had nothing to do. I felt I should be helping out with the housekeeping or something. Asur's mother saw me wandering around the back yard and asked me if I liked to read.

"We have a large library," she said. "Both Abel and I like to read, although our taste in books is quite different. I am sure with all the books we have, you'll find something you like." She showed me to the library which was a pleasant, well-lit room on one end of the house. It was quite large and shelves went all around the walls. At the far end was a large window and beneath it, small couch in which to curl up and read. In the centre of the room were a desk and chair and a couple of armchairs.

For the next few days I either sat in the library or in the shade outdoors, reading, but I soon had enough of books. What I really wanted to do was to go out and do something, or to at least feel useful around the house.

Saturday I could not go to the funeral of course, even Asur did not go, just to keep up the appearance that he was no longer on good terms with the Campanare family, but we read about it in Sunday's newspaper.

Sunday morning, I realized that I could not go to mass either. I looked at Asur in dismay. "Perhaps your friend Father Bernadi would be willing to come bring you Communion." He suggested. "Can you trust him?"

"Yes." I said. "And if he would, I would like that very much. He is at St. Gabriel's Parish now."

Father Bernardi and Asur arrived in a carriage that afternoon.

"Well!" Father Bernardi said, looking from me to Asur. "This is quite a situation! Isabella, I am willing to come bring you communion every Sunday for as long as you are here if you like."

"If you don't mind, I would like that." I replied.

"Is there a quiet place we can do this?" Father Bernardi asked Asur.

"Yes, of course. No one is in the family room right now and I can let the others know not to disturb you." Asur said.

I walked with Father Bernardi to the family room. He had brought a brief-case with him and from it pulled out a white cloth of good quality weave. It was decorated around the edges with off-white grapes and sheaves of wheat. He laid it on the little table that was in front of the couch. He then took out a small crucifix and a white candle. He placed them on the cloth and lit the candle. From his pocket, he took out a small round gold container. "This is called a pyx," he said. "It holds the blessed sacrament when we take it to the sick or shut in." He opened the pyx and laid it down on the cloth. "Ready?" he asked. I nodded. He took out his missel.

We did the sign of the cross, and the penitential rite, then he read the opening prayer and that Sunday's Gospel. We then prayed for different intentions and finished with the Our Father.

Father Bernardi took the host from the pyx, held it up and said, " This is the Lamb of God who takes away the sins of the world. Happy are those who are called to his supper."

"Lord, I am not worthy to receive you, but only say the word and I shall be healed." I answered.

"The body of Christ."

"Amen."

We prayed silently for a few minutes, then Father Bernardi read the communion prayer and blessed me, and we were done.

"Thank you so much for coming all this way to give me communion." I said. "I'm going crazy from not having anything to do nor anyone to see. I'm glad you could come. I really hated to miss mass."

"It is my pleasure." Father Bernardi said.

We went out to join the others in the back garden and chat for awhile.

"Our Bishop was not too happy to learn of your annulment." Father Bernardi told Asur and I.

"Oh no?" I asked.

"He was apparently reprimanded quite severely for participating in forcing marriage on someone. The Vatican has had complaints about him before and is considering moving him somewhere else, where he would be under someone else and in a position of less leadership."

****

Monday afternoon I noticed Asur's mother out in the garden, preparing to do some gardening. I came by to watch her.

"Can I help you Mrs. Midfallah?" I asked.

"Please, call me Meredith," she said. "And yes, I was going to weed this herb garden. Can you tell the difference between the weeds and the herbs?"

"You might want to show me." I said.

"This here is yucca glauca," she said, showing me a plant with stiff, sword-shaped leaves that were blue-green in colour. "It's common name is Adam's needle or soapweed. It grows well here although it is not from here. Because it likes dry soils. The roots of yucca glauca are good on inflammation and rheumatism. They can also be used as a laxative. I make a poultice with the roots that I use for my mother's rheumatism. One can also use it as an ingredient in shampoo. It is said to control dandruff."

"That," she said, pointing to a little plant with fuzzy, curling leaves, "is a weed. I have no use for it. It really shouldn't be too hard, I weeded last week and the week before, so most of my herbs are bigger and stronger than the weeds by now."

She moved over to another spot, "This here is called Silybum marianum or Holy thistle." She pointed to a plant with dark green shiny leaves that had scalloped edges and white spots along the veins.

"The fruit is best to use but you can use the seeds and leaves too, I use it as a stimulant and an anti-depressant although it has other uses too such as a liver tonic. And when the leaves are this young, they can be eaten as a vegetable. And here is some lavender, or Lavandula officinalis, you recognize that." I nodded.

"I use the flowers and leaves of that, and I guess you remember what for."

I smiled. "I certainly do! For magically banishing headaches!"

"If you take this part of the garden, I'll go over there and weed," she said, pointing to the left. "If in doubt, call me." She smiled.

"All right."

As the afternoon wore on, it grew hot in the garden, sweat was dripping into my eyes as I weeded and loosened the earth slightly and watered some of the plants that needed more water than others. Meredith and I chatted as we worked and I was continually amazed at her knowledge of the plant world. I was hot and tired and dirty, but I did not care. It felt great to finally be doing a little work.

"I see my mother has got you gardening."

I looked up, Asur was back from the factory.

"Watch out, she'll have you memorizing every last plant, latin *and* common names." He teased. Pointing to some plants he droned, "Amaranthus hypochondriacus, otherwise known as Lady bleeding or Prince's feather; Potentilla anserina otherwise known as Cinquefoil, Moor grass or Crampweed; Ilex paraguariensis, otherwise known as Yerba mate or Paraguay tea."

"Stop it!" laughed Meredith, getting up to greet him, "You'll have her thinking I'm some sort of horrible schoolmistress."

"Weren't you?" asked Asur. He planted a kiss on her forehead. "Hi Ma."

As I watched them, smiling, Asur left his mother and came to greet me. "You have dirt on your face." He told me. He gently rubbed my cheek and then kissed my forehead. I caught a whiff of his cologne. I closed my eyes for a second and breathed his scent in. I reopened them as he drew away.

"What's for dinner?" he asked us, "I'm starving!"

"Well," I answered, "you could always have some *Silybum marianum*, apparently the leaves are edible right now."

****

The weeks passed too quickly. I was dreading leaving the City alone. However, I was looking forward to being free once again.

"Do you want to go west to the coast or east to the continent?" Meredith asked me one day, while we were tying up bunches of herbs that were ready to dry, reminding me that soon I would have to make a choice.

"I have never been to see the sea…" I said, "I think that would be a marvelous sight." I imagined smelling salt air for the first time and seeing ships, and different kinds of people, and trees and flowers that grew everywhere. "But anywhere I go is going to be wetter than here, and greener." I thought for a minute. "Apparently there is a much greater difference in seasons on the continent. Cold in winter and hot in summer. I should like to see what it is like to be cold."

"You might not like the cold." Meredith answered.

"One of Ben Sha'rat's workers came from the continent." I remembered. "He helped put the new addition on my parents' house. He found it hard to always be working in the heat. He used to get nostalgic about his home, and he'd complain that here, there was never any cool weather to look forward to working in."

We were quiet for a moment as we bent over the last of the herbs.

"Speaking of Ben Sha'rat," Merideth said, "Did you know that Asur had heard that some people wanted him dead before he was killed?"

I shook my head in surprise.

"Asur tried to warn him, he told him what he had heard, but Ben told him he was not afraid of death and he needed to do what he had to do."

"That sounds like Ben." I said. "I guess I had it coming, didn't I? Someone like that couldn't marry and settle down and have children, someday, sooner or later, they'd have been fatherless. I guess it was just a good thing that it happened sooner." I was silent a moment. "It was good of Asur to warn him."

"Do you know why Asur warned him?" she asked me.

"No, I imagine because he wants justice for the working class as well?"

"Yes, that too." Merideth answered. "But the *main* reason Asur tried to warn Ben was because he knew you loved Ben and he wanted you to be happy."

I stared at her in shock. "He wanted me to be happy, even if it meant I would be with someone else?"

"When you love someone, sometimes you have to let them go." Meredith answered.

****

I found Asur sitting on the couch near the window in the library, reading the newspaper. He looked up as I came in. He must have noticed something in my face, because he sat up straight and asked me, "What's wrong?"

I sat down beside him and just looked at him for a minute. I took his hands in mine, "Why do you love me so, Asur?"

He was silent for a moment and looked down at our hands. Then he looked up and half-smiled at me.

"One day, back when I was about 12, Garrick Sanche was heaping insults on me because I was skinny, small, not very good in games and according to him, not worth very much at all."

"He was laughing at me with a group of other boys, saying I'd never get a girl to kiss me, and that I'd always be ugly and alone, when suddenly from out of nowhere, you marched right up to Garrick, told him *he* was the ugly one, and that the more he said ugly things, the uglier he got, and you couldn't see how any self-respecting girl in her right mind would ever want to kiss him, or even could without being sick after."

"Then you turned to me, and looked at me with those eyes of yours, so alive, so full of passion…" Asur's voice faltered. "And you said: '*I* like you Asur, you are kind and gentle, and you are *not* ugly!' Then you kissed me, right in front of them all."

"I never liked Garrick." I said vehemently.

"I got punched in the stomach for that the next day." Asur told me.

"I'm so sorry!" I said in dismay.

"Don't be." Asur said, "He couldn't do anything to me anymore. He had been proven wrong. A girl *could* like me and kiss me, even a very pretty girl like you. And that same girl found *him* disgusting."

"I was better than him, he knew it, and most importantly, I knew it, and there was nothing he could do to change that. It was just a little thing perhaps in your eyes, but it changed everything for me." Asur told me.

"You are," he paused for effect, "an amazing person. Intoxicating. The more I know about you, the more I want to know. You keep surprising me, as you did then, and it is always a pleasant surprise."

"Except perhaps at the altar." I reminded him.

"Except that, yes."

"I wish it hadn't been that way." I sighed.

I began to tremble. It started as a tiny shiver, as I opened my mouth to speak again. "You amaze me too." I half-whispered. The shivers took over and my whole body began to quiver uncontrollably. "I was so wrong about you." I tried to speak while keeping my voice from shaking. I couldn't relax. "You—you are everything I am not; strong, stable, patient and so profound."

"What's wrong?" Asur asked, concerned. "Are you cold?"

I shook my head. "No. I think…I am just…absolutely overwhelmed."

He reached for me then, pressing my head against his chest and rubbing my back until I finally relaxed again and was still.

"Since that day with Garrick I haven't been able to stop loving you." He murmured into my hair.

"And yet you could set me free." I said. Tears came to my eyes. My hands moved up to touch his face. "I have come to realize that I don't mind leaving the City behind, nor my parents, nor my friends." I said, gently stroking his chin and cheek. "They do not have a hold on me, I will miss them, but I won't be lost without them. There is only one thing, one person that I cannot bear to leave behind." Our faces had been moving closer together like magnets attracted to each other, our foreheads were now touching, and I whispered, "that person is you." I closed my eyes. I could feel his breath on my lips as he whispered "Kiss me once more."

His lips were soft and warm on mine. I sighed audibly and pulled him closer.

We stayed seated together for a long moment. I buried my nose in the hollow of his neck and breathed in his scent.

I had never noticed another person's scent before. Not like this. Sweat and perfume I had smelled before, but not this clean, basic human scent.

"You smell good." I mumbled. I could feel him shake with suppressed laughter.

"No, seriously." I said, lifting my head to meet his eyes. "I never noticed before. I like the smell of your skin."

Asur looked at me tenderly and traced a line with his finger down the bridge of my nose and across my lips. Gently he took my face in his hands and kissed me again.

"You know I can't come with you, not right now." Asur said later. We were still sitting in the library, on the couch. The sun had gone down and it was getting dark in the room. I sat leaning on Asur, my head on his shoulder, his arm around me, as we discussed our relationship. "I wish I could just drop everything and go with you, but unless you really needed me, in which case I would drop everything, I have work to do here. And I would need to put certain things in order and take care of some things before leaving permanently. "

"I know." I said. "But it still tears my heart in two to have to leave you. Especially now that I know that I love you."

"I will come to see you." Asur told me, "And maybe this time apart will just serve to strengthen our relationship. If we can get past this, then we will know that we can get past anything. Being apart will help us think about our relationship. We will be able to see more objectively. I think it will be good for us. Especially for me." He added.

"You are right, of course." We were silent for awhile. I sat, thinking about the long days ahead of me, separated from this man whom I had grown to respect and love in only a few months.

"Asur," I said, turning towards him, "I don't want to spend my life with anyone else but you. I promise to be faithful to you. I will not marry another, neither will I promise myself to another unless death separates us or you release me of my promise."

"And I," Asur said, "promise to keep loving you, to wait for you until the time comes that we can be wed."

The next day, Asur was home later than usual for supper. When he arrived, he took me aside. We went to sit down in a small garden, surrounded by small bushes on the side of the house, where we could be alone.

He took a box out of his pocket.

"I wanted to make this official," he said. He opened the box. Inside were two solid bracelets, made of gold. Asur picked up the smaller one, unclasped it and opened it. I saw then that it was hinged on the opposite side. He took my hand and put the bracelet on my wrist. All around the bracelet were sheaths of wheat, fruits and flowers, alternating with two circles entwined.

"The circles represent fidelity and the rest fruitfulness." Asur told me. "We promised each other fidelity and eventually, marriage, which we hope will bear fruit. I give you this bracelet to show that I am bound to you and you to me."

I picked up the remaining bracelet which was identical except in size, unclasped it and put it on his wrist.

"And I offer you this bracelet to show that I am bound to you and you to me by our promise."

VII

I had decided to go to the coast, to San Isidor. Meredith was with me in my room helping me to pack. Asur had brought me a couple of different magazines from San Isidor, some fashion magazines, a voyager's guide and some actuality magazines so I could get an idea of what to expect and what kinds of clothes and accessories I might need. Meredith and I were sitting on my bed scouring these magazines for details.

"It certainly seems to rain a lot on the coast." Meredith remarked. "Here in the guide it says a traveler might want to bring rain gear."

"Where would one find that here in the City?" I wondered.

"You'll probably have to find some once you get there." Meredith replied. "You should bring your umbrella with you though."

According to what information we could find, the temperature on the coast did not vary greatly during the year, because the ocean kept temperatures from rising or falling very rapidly. The difference between the average summer temperature was only about 10 degrees higher than the average winter temperature, with temperatures never rising or falling much more than 5 degrees past the average. In summer, the average was about 25 degrees Celsius and in winter it was about 15 degrees Celsius.

"Even the hottest day in San Isidor would feel like a cool breeze here." I said.

"Be careful," Asur said, coming in at that moment, "the humidity changes things. Here, it is hot but *dry*. Apparently when it is hot and *humid*, it feels like you are suffocating. Your cool day might not seem so cool after all."

"Hi Asur." I said, getting up to greet him with a kiss.

Asur greeted his mother, then turned back to me. "I brought you something," he said.

He reached into the inner pocket of the jacket he was wearing and took out a small package.

"Someone brought this to me today." Asur said. "It came from your father. There was no note, but I am sure it is for you."

I opened the package. Inside was a do-it-yourself hair colouring kit, an envelope, a pair of barber's scissors, and a small gold locket.

I tore open the envelope. Inside were bills in the international currency. Bills from the world bank are accepted anywhere. All other currency is based on the international currency. The City deals almost exclusively in international currency, while some places have preferred to keep their own currency to deal among themselves, as a matter of tradition. A letter was included in my mother's handwriting.

Dear Isabella,

One of the Peacekeepers who has been investigating your case has offered to have someone bring something to you via Asur, so we have quickly put this package together.

We know you are leaving soon and we would like you to please use the contents of this package to alter your appearance somewhat. Do it for us. Hair grows back but people do not come back from the dead.

We want you to know that we love you. We miss you greatly. We are giving you a keepsake that won't give you away. The gold locket was my grandmother's. The hair is ours.

XX Mother

My father had added "*I love you*" in his scratchy writing.

I opened the locket and saw two locks of hair, my mother's, soft and silky, and slightly wavy, with a few strands of grey on the left and my father's, mostly grey and straight on the right.

"As much as I hate to see you lose your hair," Asur said, "I think we should use the things your parents included in the package."

"She needn't cut it all off." Meredith said, "She still needs to look feminine. Her hair is so long now that shoulder length hair will change her looks enough.

One of the Midfallah's maids, a girl named Clara happened to be very good with hair. I sat in the kitchen while she chopped it off to shoulder length.

"Look, it bounces!" Clara exclaimed, obviously delighted. "It curls much better now that it is shorter and less heavy, don't you think?"

I looked in the mirror, and regretted my long hair. It didn't look quite like me anymore. Which was the point, I reminded myself.

"Yes," I agreed, "it does curl a bit more."

"I could layer it somewhat and I bet it would curl even more." Clara offered.

"It would make you look even more different." Meredith added.

"I guess so…" I said unenthusiastically.

Clara took up the scissors again.

"Not too much." I said, "I don't want it too short."

"Just a little layering, that's all." Clara reassured me.

When she was done with the scissors, she got the hair colouring kit ready.

"This is going to make your hair a fair bit lighter," Meredith said, "but at least your mother has taste. It isn't going to make you so blonde it looks fake, more like a light brown."

When I looked into the mirror again, I gasped. The layers had made my hair quite a bit lighter and therefore much curlier. With the light brown hair the way I looked was totally changed. It didn't look bad, but it was going to take some getting used to.

A female peacekeeper in plain clothes came a couple of days later to get a picture of me to put on my passport. She handed me a pair of eyeglasses. "Put these on." She told me, before taking the picture, from now on you will wear glasses. Don't worry, they are not prescription eyewear. They won't hurt your eyes. It is just a further disguise."

"We have contacts in San Isidor who have rented an apartment for you." She informed me. They know nothing about your real identity. Only the person who will be living with you has any information on your case. It is safer that way. Your name will be Rosa Martin. That is all they know. If anyone asks, your parents were originally from Hispania, but you were born and raised in the City. Your parents are both dead. You are middle class, your father owned a small business, which, since his death, has been sold and you are coming to San Isidor to study and hopefully eventually support yourself in some way. That is all anyone needs to know. Try not to get into details with anyone about your background, otherwise it will become too complicated and details like names could be verified by anyone suspicious of your identity. Change the subject instead."

I nodded.

"A carriage will come for you next Monday to take you to the shuttle." The peacekeeper told me. "A peacekeeper will travel with you, posing as your brother. Other peacekeepers will also be in the shuttle, undercover. The peacekeeper who is to travel with you will have your passport. He will be traveling under the name Leo Martin."

"Thank you." I said.

"It is our job." The peacekeeper smiled. She looked at my clothes. "You will have to find some clothes that do not shout 'I am high class' to the world. Your clothes may be simple, but they are still high quality, of good cut and costly material. You will need something a little cheaper, but not too cheap."

I gave Clara some money, as she and I were of a similar build and she went into town to buy just a couple of new outfits, pretending to be buying them for herself. Clara had good taste and, although our style was not exactly the same, I was satisfied with the clothes she brought back. There were two long skirts, one dark brown, the other beige, a light tan chemise with a tiny bit of lace at the collar, a white chemise in a similar style, a sleeveless beige knit top whose only decoration was in the contrasting stitches and a dark brown jacket in a nice flattering cut. Clara had obviously chosen the clothes with care to make sure I would be able to mix and match them.

"These are wonderful." I told her. "You did a great job. You have excellent taste. Thanks."

"You're welcome." Clara smiled. "We should go through your clothes. Some of them, a middle-class girl might wear. The rest, you'll have to leave here, but once you get to where you are going, you can always buy more clothes."

****

Late Sunday morning, Father Bernadi came to give me communion for the last time.

"I wish you well," he said before leaving to prepare for afternoon mass. "Know that you will be in my prayers."

"Thank you." I replied.

He reached into the folds of his cassock and drew out something small. He opened his hand and I could see that it was a small pendant and chain.

"This is the sword of the archangel Michael," he said, giving it to me. "May you be ever under his protection."

I took the pendant in my hand and saw that indeed it was a fiery sword, hanging with the blade pointing to the ground and the hilt, with it's cross-guard, at the top, so that it also looked somewhat like a cross hanging from the chain.

"Thank you." I said again, putting the chain around my neck. "You have been a wonderful friend, I will miss you greatly."

"And I, you."

I hugged him and let him go. Asur put his arm around me as we watched him go out the gate and turn the corner to catch a carriage back to his parish.

I spent my last afternoon in the Midfallah estate alone with Asur in one of the gardens. We did not talk much, we were content just to be together.

I had a hard time falling asleep that night. I was anxious about the journey ahead, and already my heart ached for home and for Asur.

****

I finished dressing for the last time in the room that had been mine during my short stay at the Midfallah estate. I peered into the mirror at the image of myself with very wavy shoulder length, light brown hair. I was wearing the knit top with the beige skirt, which, although very flattering, were quite different from clothes I was used to wearing. I saw the glasses lying on the commode in front of me and slipped them on. Immediately, any last resemblance to myself that the image in the mirror might have had disappeared. A stranger stared back at me.

Book Two

I

I blinked back the tears as I saw the carriage pull up at the Midfallah estate for me. I could no longer speak. Asur pulled me closer to him, and his parents, having already said goodbye to me, left us to give us some privacy.

"I will always be here for you." Asur murmured. "Do not cry. Think of it as an adventure. You will see many new things and meet new people. You will explore a new culture and new ways. It can be an exciting time if you will."

I nodded.

"You are in my heart," Asur told me looking into my eyes, "and I am in yours. You have only to look there, in your heart, to see me. And somehow, we will find a way to communicate."

"I know," I whispered, "I will be strong."

"Go now," he said. "They are waiting." He kissed me, one last lingering kiss.

I turned to step into the carriage. The man inside, a peacekeeper I knew, although he was dressed in plain clothes, smiled a sympathetic smile.

I looked behind me for as long as I could still see the Midfallah estate. The man across from me was silent, somehow knowing I needed some time to myself.

As we came closer to the markets and the opening to the Passage, I started to feel calmer inside. The man must have sensed this because he leaned slightly towards me and smiled a warm smile.

"Good morning Rosa," he said. "I am your brother Leo Martin." He winked. "I will be accompanying you to San Isidor."

I immediately liked this man, whose real name I would probably never know. I smiled back at him. "Nice to meet you, brother." I replied.

In many ways, our world has reverted to primitive means. In the City, everyone walks, even the high classes, unless it is really too far to walk, and then we get a carriage, drawn by horses. Long gone are the days when people polluted the air with many gas-run vehicles. One reason is that pollution levels grew too high for comfort, but the main reason is that finally, we simply ran out of fuel. Electricity we still have because that is a renewable energy and does not pollute the air as others fuels do. Our scientists have become experts in all things renewable. Our water is used and purified and re-used, otherwise the City simply would not survive. Water is precious here, in such an arid place. It was here that the process of water purification was perfected.

Renewable resources that require little or no refining are also used in the building of homes and other things. Goods are often transported through the passage on camels, although this is reserved for non-perishable items, as it is a slow method of transportation.

In other ways however, our world is very advanced. I believe our forefathers would have been convinced that we possessed magic. Sometimes, I myself, am half convinced that I am witnessing magic.

While goods are sometimes transported by camel, most people who are going any good distance take a shuttle. I had never been in a shuttle before, as I had never left the City before. I realized, as I grew closer to the shuttle port, that I was excited to be finally embarking in a shuttle.

A shuttle, of all things in our world, seems to me to be the most magical. One enters into the oval—shaped shuttle, the shuttle lowers itself into what seems to be a hole in the ground, and in a very short time, one finds himself disembarking in a faraway land.

I found I was nervous as I entered the shuttle. Inside were plush seats around the walls and in the center. Chrome and wood accents decorated the walls. The floor of the shuttle was carpeted. Works of art depicting scenes from different countries decorated the walls. I especially liked one of cascading falls and lush greenery. Rays of sunlight peered through mist and leaves, it seemed so alive, so magical. It was unlike anything I had ever known in my dry, dry world.

Leo and I sat down side by side on one side of the shuttle. Slowly the shuttle filled up with a number of different people.

When everyone was inside, the doors were shut by the attendant. The shuttle then started to descend, then stopped.

What happened next was a bizarre sensation of falling, yet that does not describe it. It was as if we had become as weightless as a beam of light and were hurtling into space. Almost as soon as it had started, it stopped and the shuttle ascended. The attendant opened the doors.

"This is not our stop." Leo murmured to me. "We are only half way. This is Al Atiraca. We are still over five hundred kilometres from the coast. We are not even in Hispania yet."

Al Atiraca, I remembered, was only a small city. But since it was at a crossroads, and halfway to the City from San Isidor, it had a shuttle port. Shuttle ports were rare, mostly only the largest, most important cities had them, because they were so expensive and hard to build. People generally traveled by carriage to the nearest port, took the shuttle and then traveled the rest of the way by carriage again. Passage on the shuttles was also quite expensive, so often people went all the way by carriage.

Some passengers had stepped out and now more were coming in. The attendant closed the doors again and the shuttle descended. Once again I felt the weightless sensation and then the shuttle began to rise again.

Leo got up as the attendant opened the doors. I rose with him, as did everyone else. As soon as we approached the door, the hot humid air hit me. It was like walking into a sauna. I had never experienced humidity like this before. My clothes stuck to my skin, I found breathing difficult. I knew it could not be quite as hot as in the City, but it seemed hotter. There was no wind and I waved my hand in front of my face, but that did not change much. I turned around and looked at the panorama before me.

We were still outside the city of San Isidor, ports are always built outside city limits. All around us were trees, huge, tall, leafy trees. The vegetation was lush and thick. There were bushes and flowers and grass and vines. It seemed that green things were vying for every spot available. Here and there I could see some buildings through the trees.

Leo took my arm. "Come," he said. "We are expected."

I picked up my valise and he led me towards a carriage.

"Hola," he said to the driver.

"Hola." The driver answered back.

That was when it hit home that these people also had another language, one I did not understand. Most people spoke the international language, the language spoken by everyone in the City, but like currency, although everyone accepted the international currency, some places still had their own money, and some places also had their own language.

Leo helped me up into the carriage, said a few more words to the driver and then sat down beside me.

"Your apartment is in the old part of San Isidor, near the bay." He told me.

We headed through streets lush with trees and vines and the scent of flowers hung sweet and heavy in the air. Spanish moss hung from many trees and vines grew all over many of the oldest of the houses we passed by.

The farther along we went, the more crowded the houses were, and the more people there were in the streets, talking, laughing, most of it in this language that I did not understand.

We finally pulled up in front of a house that was 3 stories high and that had been converted into 6 apartments. Huge trees that I did not know the name of stood in front of the building, shading it from the sun. Some tenants had flower boxes on their balconies.

"This is it!" Leo told me. "Apartment 5. The bay is right down that way." He added, pointing behind the buildings on the other side of the street. "There is a boardwalk not far from here that follows the shore for awhile. Really nice."

I followed Leo inside the building and up the stairs. He stopped at the door with a number 5 on it and knocked. From inside the apartment we could hear the sound of footsteps coming to the door. The lock in the door turned and then the door opened. A very attractive young woman stood in the doorway.

She had dark skin and dark eyes, lined with thick lashes and a lovely mouth with full lips. Her nose was slightly round and pert and her hair was very dark, thick and wavy.

"Hoooola Leo!" She said with a rich deep voice, obviously very happy to see him.

"Que tal Leticia!" Leo answered. They kissed each other briefly once on each cheek. "How are you? This is my sister Rosa." He winked. Obviously Leticia knew that I was not really his sister.

"How are you Rosa?" Leticia greeted me warmly, with a slight accent, and kissing me on both cheeks as well. I was slightly taken aback, as in the city this is not a custom among strangers, but I did not let it show.

"Come in! Come in!" Leticia was saying in her lovely low voice. We entered the apartment.

We were standing in a small salon with plants in pots here and there and a couple of paintings on the wall. There were glass sliding doors opposite the door we had just come through, leading outside to the balcony. To my right was a corridor leading to other parts of the apartment.

"I did not do much decorating yet," Leticia told me, "I was waiting for you, perhaps you have some things to add too?"

"Oh, but this is lovely." I said.

A fan on the ceiling was twirling, making the heat easier to support. The floors were hardwood and the walls were painted a pale lilac colour.

"Come, I will show you the rest of the apartment." Leticia said.

****

I lay down on the single bed in my new room about an hour later, after Leo had left. I had excused myself to Leticia, saying that I wanted to unpack, get settled and rest a bit. She told me she had to go out and do some errands anyway, so she was going to leave for the market.

The room was smaller than any I had ever slept in before, but it was adequate. I had seen worse. The floor was also hardwood. There was a fan hanging off the ceiling here too, and a large window which looked out onto the street below. The walls here were white except for wood accents. Huge wooden beams crossed the ceiling, the door frame was wood and so was the border going around the room. It was very simple but had a lot of charm. There were white curtains at the windows.

I had finished putting what I had brought with me into the dresser. I had practically nothing to put into the desk that was also in the room. The problem was the bed. I had not brought any sheets, pillows or covers. The bed had a mattress and nothing more.

I closed my eyes. I recalled Asur's face as he was telling me to think of it as an adventure and I wanted to cry. I had not asked for adventure. I only wanted to be back at home, with those I loved.

I touched the bracelet around my wrist gently with my thumb, tracing the sheaves of wheat, thinking of the man who had given it to me.

I finally fell asleep.

II

"...studies of cases have shown that when dealing with children in unstable families,..." The professor droned on. I shifted on my chair, trying to find a more comfortable position and at the same time, trying not to fall asleep. It was not that the subject was boring, just that the professor seemed to have no life, and to make matters worse, this course started at 3:00 in the afternoon, and that is when I always seem to start to get sleepy.

Not long after arriving in San Isidor, I had signed up for a degree in Social Services at the University of San Isidor. I had to do something, but I was not qualified for anything, so I thought studying would be the best thing. Arrangements were made and I entered university. Since this was an international university, courses were given in the international language, understanding would not be a problem for me.

I had also signed up for a beginning course in Castellano, the national language of Hispaña.

"...I want you to find a partner..." the professor was saying now, "...you will work as a team, choosing a specific case file and describing how you would deal with the different situations..."

I groaned inside. I knew no one, how would I find a partner. I looked at the girl to my left, she was already making plans with another on her other side. I looked to the right, it was the same. Directly in front of me, everyone already seemed to have a partner.

I felt something jab me in the back. I jumped and turned around.

A young woman with red hair and green eyes was smiling at me. "Do you have a partner?" she asked.

"No." I replied, "Do you want to be mine?"

"Good!" she exclaimed, "Great! I thought I'd never find one, everyone else seems to have one."

"Me neither." I said smiling.

"My name's Erin Owen."

"And I am Rosa Martin." I replied.

"So, where do you want to meet to do this." Erin asked me.

"Maybe we should start with the library." I suggested. "To find a case file to study."

"Good idea, and then we could look at it from my place. It isn't very far, I live with my sister and her family." Erin told me.

"They wouldn't mind me going there?" I asked

"Oh no, you'll see, they like people, they like having people over."

"Ok then." I said

****

I awoke in the middle of the night and sat straight up in bed, my heart was pounding. Slowly I realized that the horrible sound that had woken me was only the hissing and squalling of the neighbour's cat fighting with another one. My heart slowly left my throat, went back to its rightful place, and started to beat less rapidly.

I turned over in bed. I had been to buy sheets and a few covers, but all that was really needed were sheets. It was too hot and humid for anything else. Even with the fan going at maximum overhead, I was still hot and uncomfortable. My hair stuck to the back of my neck like it had never done in the City. Sweat pooled in the small of my back. I could not get back to sleep.

I started to think of my family, of Asur and I felt so lonely. It had been a month since I was here and I had not had any news of them. I could not write them either because it was considered to be too dangerous for the moment.

I touched the bracelet around my wrist and thought of Asur. I imagined seeing him again, being free again to be myself, to wear my hair long and dark again, which reminded me I had to find a hairdresser soon to take care of the dark hair at the roots that had grown since I had coloured it.

I turned again. I sighed. If only those who wanted to kill me could be apprehended, if only Asur could be with me. If only…

I started up at the ceiling. I had to stop thinking like this. It would only be awhile before I could have my life back. I would get my degree in social studies and by then I would surely be able to go back, and Asur and I could be together again and be involved in change for the better.

****

It was a half-hour walk to the university, and one that I enjoyed very much. Most of the way I walked through residential areas, full of old homes and huge trees spreading their branches to form a canopy over the sidewalks. Often in the mornings I would pass children going to a neighbourhood school or a milkman, letter-carrier or newspaper deliverer as well as other people walking to work or other daily occupations. The last ten minutes of my trajectory was in a more commercial area, with many shops, boutiques, restaurants and the occasional pub or café.

The University was in the center of the business sector of the old city. Its wide green spaces and large pavilions broke up the monotony of red or grey brick business buildings. It was like a huge park. One always saw students lounging under trees, reading or talking. People often went to picnic there. It was a beautiful place, clean and well kept.

On Avenida San Martin, the large boulevard that went past the University and that crossed over half the city, I had begun to stop at a small café about 5 minutes away from the University for a cup of coffee that I would then take with me to class in a special insulated cup that came with a cover that I had bought for that reason. It was called Café Esperanza.

The birds were singing in the trees as I headed towards the door of the café, and the sun was already bright with the promise of another hot day although the air was not unbearable yet this early in the morning. There was a slight breeze that tugged at my hair, and kept things reasonably cool.

I could hear the murmur of voices as I entered the café. Many people stopped here for a coffee before heading on to wherever they were going. Many of them were students like me. The huge windows of the café were wide open, letting in the breeze and the noise from the street.

I stood in line to order my coffee. They make the best coffee I have ever tasted here, rich in taste and strong, yet not bitter.

A street musician appeared at the street corner and I watched him set up a spot to play. He unfolded a three-legged stool and opened his violin case. Gently, he withdrew the violin and bow and placed them delicately against the stool. Next he placed the open violin case in front of him so people could throw money into it as they passed by.

He carefully picked up his violin and caressed it as one does a precious object. He settled it on his shoulder and nestled his chin against it. He picked up his bow and set it on the violin. He closed his eyes. I realized I was holding my breath in expectation and that I was no longer paying attention to the line in front of me, there was open space between myself and the person in front of me. I moved up, closing the gap and turned around to watch the violinist again.

He opened his eyes and started to play. The strains of a tune, melancholic, pleading, entered the café. I strained to hear them above the noise of people talking and laughing.

"¿Señora?" I heard the lady behind the counter address me.

"Oh!" I said turning around. "Sorry, uh…disculpame."

"What can I get you?" Asked the lady with a thick accent.

"Un cappuccino por favor." I said hesitantly. I handed her my cup so she could fill it up. When she came back with it, I paid her and turned around to go back outside.

As I was exiting the café, someone bumped into to me from behind, causing me to almost lose my balance. My book bag fell from my shoulder, hit the cup in my hand and my coffee fell to the ground, the cover came off and the coffee spilled all over the sidewalk.

I stood there momentarily in shock staring at the coffee staining the sidewalk, then slowly bent down to retrieve my cup.

A hand quickly stopped me. A young man came from behind me to pick up my cup.

"I am so sorry," he said, standing up to face me, with the cup and cover in his hands. "Let me buy you another one."

"Oh, that's okay, you don't have to do that." I replied quickly.

"I insist." The man said, "I bumped into you, causing you to spill all your coffee and you probably hadn't even had a sip of it yet. I will feel very badly if you do not let me buy you another one."

"All right then." I said, smiling.

He visibly relaxed and smiled back.

"You were not hurt?" he inquired, "You did not get burned?"

"Oh, no!" I assured him quickly, "It all fell on the ground."

I lined up again behind the young man who was still holding my cup in his hand. I turned around again to watch the violinist play.

"He is very good, is he not?" The young man said from behind me.

I turned around to face him. "Yes."

"He often plays in the Mercado," the man told me, "This is the first time I've seen him here."

The violinist finished the piece and started another. The music was sad, the soft high notes made me feel sad too.

"What do I order for you?" the young man asked.

"Oh," I replied, "I had a cappuccino."

The lady behind the counter rinsed my cup out for me and re-filled it. The young man ordered himself a coffee as well and we walked out of the café together.

"Thank you very much." I said.

"Not a problem. Would you like to meet the violinist? I happen to know him."

"Sure." I said.

"I don't even know your name."

"Oh, sorry, it's Rosa."

"Ignacius."

"Pleased to meet you." I held out my hand.

"My pleasure." He replied, taking my hand briefly.

We walked closer to the violinist, who finished his piece and laid down his violin.

"¡Ignacius! Que placer verte de nuevo!"

"Hola David. I told this lady I would introduce you, she seems to enjoy your music very much. Her name is Rosa. This is David," he said turning to me. "The best violin player in San Isidor."

David laughed. "Do not listen," he said, "he exaggerates."

I suddenly remembered that I had a course I was supposed to be going to. In horror I looked at my watch and saw that I had five minutes to get there. I was going to have to run.

"I'm so sorry." I said quickly, "I don't mean to leave like this, but I'm going to be late for my course, I really have to run. Maybe I'll see you around again? If you're here often?"

"We will definitely make plans to be here more often from now on." David winked at me.

I smiled back, hurriedly said goodbye and started to half walk, half run in the direction of the university.

III

I was meeting Erin at her sister's house so we could do some case studies together. I was a little late, so I half-ran, half-walked through the quiet streets. To me, they seemed quiet, although the natives might not have thought so. The huge trees and thick vegetation everywhere tended to muffle sound, so even though here, too, children played in the street or in back yards, and housewives hummed to themselves as they hung the laundry out to dry, it did not seem as loud as in The City. Of course, people in The City, most of them being merchants born of merchants, born of merchants, tended to always be loud, even when they were not bargaining or selling and were only greeting you. I had started to make a conscious effort to keep my voice softer, otherwise people started to stare at me.

Erin greeted me at the door and invited me to follow her to the kitchen at the back of the house. Erin's sister, Maria was at the stove cooking what looked to be some kind of soup or stew. She turned around and smiled.

"Would you like something to drink?" she asked.

"Oh yes, thank you. I'm drier than a gecko at midday!" I replied.

"A what?" Maria looked confused.

Erin laughed. "I love the expressions you come up with Rosa. "They're so colourful."

"But I didn't come up with it, it's quite common really." I protested.

"Not here it isn't." Erin laughed again.

"What is a gay-co?" Maria asked.

"A gecko? Oh of course, I suppose you wouldn't have any around here." I smiled, feeling foolish. "It's a kind of lizard."

****

Erin and I moved to the living room to work on our case studies, as the kitchen was getting crowded and boisterous with the supper preparations, and two of Maria's three children doing homework.

I stayed for supper, which was very lively with the children. Gabriela, age 11, with long dark wavy hair, looked the most different of the three. Although I could see that she shared the shape of her nose, long and narrow, with her mother and her youngest brother. The other two children were slightly lighter in complexion, their hair was straight and lighter as well. Gabriela joked with the adults, with a subtleness that the other two did not quite get.

Ian was the second child, a vivacious 7 year old, ready to play pranks on his younger brother, which weren't always welcomed. Ian had beautiful green eyes which looked out from under dark, thick eyelashes. He had the same auburn hair as his mother and his aunt, and a dash of freckles across his nose. He was slender, like Gabriela.

Roberto was the youngest child, only 4, and like Gabriela, had light brown, almost hazel eyes. His hair was straight, like Ian's, but much less red. He seemed to be built a bit more solidly than the other two, and was more serious.

Ian had wisked Roberto's dessert from his place while Roberto was not looking and had hid it and Roberto was complaining loudly. Maria was admonishing both of them, when her husband came in.

"Un poco de silencio por favor!" He growled. The boys instantly sat up and were quiet.

The man entered the dining room.

"Hola Alberto." Maria said, getting up from her chair to serve him. "This is Rosa, a friend of Erin's from the University. They are studying together."

"Hello." Alberto greeted me with a slight accent. "Welcome to our home."

"Thank you." I replied.

I could see where Roberto's stocky figure had come from. Alberto had large shoulders. He wasn't extremely tall, only a few inches higher than me, but he looked quite strong. He had straight, medium brown hair and a firm jaw-line.

Alberto Morales had a very dry sense of humour and kept us laughing for the rest of the meal with his stories.

It was starting to get late when I left to go back to my apartment. The dew had already fallen and the smell of nighttime, a humid smell of rotting leaves and fanning flowers, cut grass and barbecues, called asados here, permeated the air. I could hear voices in backyards talking and laughing together after a long day. Some people sat on their front porches nodding at those who walked by.

"Adios." They would say if our eyes met.

"Adios." I replied. I was getting used to this form of salutation, even though the idea of using that expression as a casual greeting was very strange to me. Basically it meant "Till God" and I had only heard it before in cases when one would never see the other again.

I was not walking very quickly, as I was enjoying the cooler air that night brought. It gets quite hot in San Isidor, but it is the humidity that makes things unbearable. There seemed to be a good breeze off the bay coming in as well, which did not often happen, even though the University and the area I lived in were not too far from the water's edge. The many islands in the bay separate San Isidor from the open ocean and therefore strong winds do not always penetrate the sheltered bay.

It was when I passed a small canteen, which sold pieces of chicken, empanadas and tortillas, a variety of salads, as well as beer and soda, that I noticed a short, bald man seated on one of the bar stools at the counter. He was not looking at me, but rather reading a newspaper. A full glass of beer was on the counter in front of him.

He looked familiar. However, I could not place him. I was certain I had seen him somewhere before, maybe even more than once, without really noticing him until now.

He looked up from the newspaper and saw me looking at him. He frowned, rubbed his short moustache with one hand, folded up his newspaper and turned around to talk to the canteen owner.

I walked past, still glancing at him from time to time, trying to figure out where I had seen him before, and then I suddenly realized that he looked very much like a typical man from The City.

It isn't that men from the city and men from San Isidor are so different. Some are, but people from The City tend to be a mixture of many races, and although this is not exclusive to The City by any means, it is typical of it. This man had a large nose, although not wide like some black people, and what hair he had was slightly curly. He also had large lips and a medium complexion. It was his eyes that stood out. When he had looked at me, I noticed that they were a grayish green. This contrasted sharply with his complexion.

I was almost certain that he was from The City, but I had never met him before. I glanced back at him one more time, and saw him watching me. He turned away again quickly.

I walked on and pushed thoughts of the man to the back of my mind. I wanted to enjoy the rest of the walk back to my apartment.

As I reached Avenida San Martin, the sidewalk grew slightly more crowded. Many people sat in terraces in front of cafes or pubs, or were strolling around, enjoying the evening. I crossed the busy avenue, turned left, and continued walking.

At the corner of Avenida San Martin and Ruta de la Patria, I turned right. De la Patria goes towards the Bay for several hundred meters, then turns towards the left and meanders through a very residential sector of the city. My apartment was not very far from here, only a couple of blocks and just over a five minute walk away.

By the time I got home, Leticia was already in bed. I needed to finish writing up my case studies for the next morning, so I quietly went to my room and opened my PCD (Personal Communications Device), which is a com system and portable computer plus a few other options all in one. It is about the size and weight of a large book. The com system receiver plugs into the top. To answer or to call, one simply pushes a button and it snaps out. The com system comes complete with video and still camera as well as a radio and a digital music player. The radio or music player automatically shuts off when a call comes in and turns back on once the call is over.

The rest of the PCD opens up like a book, with a screen on one side and a keyboard on the other for writing documents, and any number of other uses, such as games, or art and photography, or music. All this and it runs on only one fusion crystal. I had bought it at the start of the school year and it was the latest in communications technology, or comtec as the field was often called now.

The PCD is of course, connected to the net. I was going to finish writing up my case study tonight, so I could send it to my professor through the net the next day.

It may seem that we have technologically regressed in terms of transportation, aside from the portals, but communication technology has advanced so much that the need to travel has been greatly reduced. In fact, most people do not travel much outside of their general neighbourhood except for pleasure trips.

Most things needed for daily life are made or grown locally, it is the luxury items or items only found in a specific region that are imported or exported.

Before settling down to finish writing up the case study, I decided to check up on news from the City over the net.

The big headlines were all about the latest raise in transportation fees. The merchants didn't like this because it meant that the price of their goods would have to go up, which would have an effect on the number of buyers. I skimmed over this and past the numerous society articles. I wasn't interested in who had been to dine with whom.

I was about to leave the newspaper when I came across the following headline:

MURDERER OF CAMPANARE SERVANT LINKED TO PROMINENT MERCHANT

Investigations into the murder of the Campanare servant, Filonia Connaught have led peacekeepers to believe that the murderer may have been hired by one of the city's prominent merchants, many of whom were not happy with some of Isabella Campanare's social justice activities.

Some rumors have it that the very family that Isabella married into, before obtaining an annulment, may have had something to do with the murder,...

"What!?" I could not help exclaiming aloud. That was impossible. How could anybody be blaming them? I certainly hoped my parents were not.

...but peacekeepers refuse to confirm this rumor.

"I should hope not!" I snorted to myself.

The detective in charge of the case, Kalim Malid was unavailable for commentary.

I decided to question Leticia about the matter the next morning to see if she knew anything more.

****

Rays of sunlight were pouring into the kitchen the next morning, where I sat, sipping coffee from a ceramic mug shaped in the form of a cat, my PCD in front of me. I was almost done reviewing what I had finished writing the night before and I was about to send it to my professor. I had no classes that morning, but two in the afternoon and I was going to head out to the hairdresser's to touch up on my dark roots.

Leticia walked out of her room and came into the kitchen, stretching and yawning.

"¿Café?" I asked.

"Por favor, ¡sí!"

I reached behind me to the cupboard where the coffee mugs and other dishes were kept, pulled out a huge pink one that was covered in roses, and poured her a cup from the carafe on the counter.

"It is a beautiful day, no?" said Leticia in her slight accent, which made it sound more like "Eet ees a bee-yoo-tee-full day, no?"

I agreed.

"Leticia," I said, "I saw an article in the City Herald last night, about the murder case. It said that the murderer had been linked to a prominent merchant, but they didn't know which one yet. But some people were spreading rumours that it might be the Midfallah family. That's ridiculous!"

"Ahh." Said Leticia. "Yes, the murderer was hired by a merchant, that much we do know. But Detective Malid has a pretty good idea which one it is, he just doesn't have proof right now."

"I see." I paused. "Do you know who it might be?"

Leticia smiled. "I am not at liberty to discuss it."

"But why are there rumors about the Midfallahs? Surely they had nothing to do with the matter!"

"I believe it was your, ah, friend Asur who thought that it would be a good idea to spread such rumors so as to keep the real suspect from believing that he is under investigation."

"Ah." Something told me that Asur knew more than I about the case.

****

By the time my last class of the day had ended, I was starting to feel quite tired. I decided to head over to the Café Esperanza to study for a bit at one of the tables, with a good espresso at hand.

I chose a table outside on the patio, beside a huge pot of flowers. The delicate smell of the flowers mixed with the smell of coffee and other smells off the street as I breathed in. There was a constant chattering and laughing in the background.

I opened my PCD and started reviewing notes for my Introduction to Social Studies class. Mid-term exams were not far off and I wanted to get a good start on studying.

I had gotten half-way through the notes, and had finished a short assignment for the class, when I noticed that the melancholic chords of a violin had joined in the background noise of the café.

I looked up and saw David standing where I had seen him the first time, a few weeks earlier, playing his violin.

I stayed an hour longer at the table, studying and organizing my courses. It was getting dark, so I started to put my things away. David played his last piece of music, and gathered up the coins that people had thrown into his violin case.

I put my PCD along with a few paper books and my now empty cup into my school bag and took a coin out of my purse. Getting up off my chair, I walked over to where David was putting away his instrument.

"Hi." I said.

He looked up. "Hello."

"We met a few weeks ago." I reminded him. "I was with Ignacius."

"Oh, yes of course." He straightened up, took my hand and kissed me on both cheeks. "How are you?"

"Quite well." I replied. "Studying for exams. I enjoy your music, it helps me to relax and concentrate."

"I am glad," he said. "I will play for you any day!"

I added my coin to the pile of other ones.

"How long have you been playing?" I asked.

"I have played the violin for 5 years now."

"Just five? You are very good."

"Thank you. But I have played other instruments before." He replied.

"Oh, which ones?"

"Guitar, accordion, a bit of piano. I have been playing since I was a child," he said.

David put the coins into his pocket and took his violin case in hand.

"Do you play here often?" I asked him.

"I do now." He answered. "But I have not been in San Martin for a very long time. I was gone for 12 years. I have just come back. This place," he said, indicating the street, "It has changed since I left 12 years ago. It is much more lively now. More people. A good place for a musician to come play his music."

"So you'll be back." I smiled.

"Definitely."

"Then I hope to see you again, and hear you play." I told him.

David smiled and bowed. "It will be my honour," he said.

IV

San Isidor is next to the ocean, which means that temperatures from one season to the next never differ much more than 10 degrees or so. It is always warm and humid, even now that we were heading into winter. The days were getting shorter, but they were still warm, although not as stifling as they were when I first arrived.

Mid-terms had passed and Christmas was coming again. It had now been almost 6 months since I had left the City. Some days it seemed like I had dreamed up the City and Asur and my parents. I was in a new world and the old one was so far away.

I started to sleep with blankets at night because the nights were definitely cooler.

I came home from a morning course at the university one day, and Leticia met me with a letter. I recognized the writing at once. It was from Asur.

Dear Rosa, it read, *I hope this finds you well.*

As your brother Leo was recently passing through, I decided to take advantage of the fact to send you a small note.

Please do not worry about things you may see in the news. Everything is under control.

I trust we will see each other sooner than later.

I miss you.

It was unsigned and the *I miss you* was tacked on to the end like he thought it was a bad idea, but couldn't help himself anyway. I smiled at that thought, even though I thought the note was hopelessly short and would have liked to have received a whole epistle.

****

I was studying again with Erin one Sunday afternoon, a few weeks before exams and Christmas holidays. Erin stretched and declared that she needed a break.

"I have something I need to go and pick up." She told me, "I won't be long."

"Alright." I replied, lifting the hair off my neck, where it was sticking, because of the humidity. We were sitting in the screened back porch, under the shade of a few trees, enjoying what little breeze there was.

I wandered into the kitchen where Maria was just getting herself a glass of juice.

"Would you like some juice?" she asked me.

"Oh, yes please." I replied, suddenly realizing that I was rather thirsty.

We sat down at the kitchen table together, where a ceiling fan was valiantly trying to create the semblance of a fresh breeze.

I ran my fingers through my hair, at the nape again.

"It's very humid today." I complained.

"Yes."

Maria took a sip of her juice.

"Where are the children?" I inquired.

"Ian and Roberto have gone to market with their father and Gabriela is upstairs reading."

Maria shook her head. "That man!" She said.

I looked at her inquisitively.

"He has gone to get wood and materials to build a garden bench. His mother is coming to visit for the Christmas holidays, and he wants a nice bench so she can sit outside in style, and enjoy the garden."

"That's nice." I said.

She looked straight at me. "Yes," she said, "it is. I would find it nice too, except that I have been telling him for a very long time that I would like a place to store the children's outdoor toys, so that they are not in the cold room, where we keep the vegetables and fruit, but he will not build that. We don't have money for simple box with a lid, that could always double as a seat, but we have money to build a fancy garden bench for a woman who will be here for no more than a week."

"Ah…" I said.

"He's not the one who cleans up after them, nor has to get past toys to get to the food every day, or I am sure he would have put it at the top of his priorities." Maria continued. "Sometimes it seems that my needs always come second to his. If a thing is on his list of priorities, then it gets done. If it is something that bothers mostly me, then it doesn't get done. Or it takes a very long time to get done."

"That has to be frustrating." I said.

"Extremely frustrating." She replied. "And if I keep asking, then I am nagging." She sighed. "But he is still a good husband. He does a lot for his family."

"Hmmm." I replied.

The back door opened at that moment, and Erin came in, with a small package in her hand.

"Just taking this upstairs," she said, "I'll be right down, save some of that juice for me!"

"I like your advent wreath." I told Maria, fingering the beautiful pink and purple ribbons that were placed around an evergreen wreath, along with flowers and berries. It was sitting on the table, with 3 purple candles, one pink one and one tall white candle in the middle. The purple and pink were for the four weeks of Advent, or the four weeks before Christmas, and the white one was to be lit at Christmas, representing the Christ child.

"Thank you." Maria said. "I like to do things like this with my children. Alberto thinks it is useless, but I think it will bring a bit of life to their faith."

"He thinks it is useless?"

"Alberto is,…" Maria stopped, trying to think how best to describe what she wanted to say.

"Alberto is very pragmatic." Erin interrupted, coming back downstairs to join us at the table.

"Yes," Maria agreed. "Philosophical things, are not,…his way."

"But, faith is very philosophical." I said. "Does he not, believe?"

"Oh, yes." Maria said. "But to know that God exists, that he created the world, etc, etc, that is enough. He does not care to reflect on it, and he does not see the need for all these symbols and extra signs of faith."

"I see." I said.

"He is the ultimate male." Erin laughed suddenly. "If you have a practical problem, he will fix it, but do not ask him to reflect on why it happened, or listen to how it makes you feel."

"Oh no!" Maria laughed, shaking her head. "Absolutely not! I think he is afraid of emotion. I think he has succeeded for so long in suppressing emotion that now it is as if he had none. So he does not understand why others should have any. Emotions are alien things to him and he does not know how to deal with them."

"Poor Gabriela." Erin said. "Now that she is entering adolescence, Alberto has no idea how to approach her anymore." Her laughter pealed out loud. "Female hormones and all."

****

Erin and Maria had invited me to spend Christmas with them. Since Leticia had other plans, and would not be alone at Christmas, I accepted.

Christmas started in Maria and Alberto's house with a solemn lighting of the advent wreath, with the tall, white one in the centre, now being lit as well. Then Maria read the story of the first Christmas. The children laid shoes out for St Nicolas, who would come around while they were at Christmas mass, and everyone trooped out.

The church we went to was lit with hundreds of candles. No other lighting was used. It was beautiful. At the front of the church, a huge, although not life-sized, stable had been set up and statues representing Mary, Joseph, the donkey, the cow, and baby Jesus in the manger had been placed inside. A few sheep peered around the corner and one could see shepherds just behind.

We filed into a pew about halfway up the aisle, and Ian and Roberto started to shove each other, both full of excitement. Alberto grabbed each boy by one arm and separated them. They were instantly quiet.

Gabriela stood between Alberto's mother and me, looking very pretty in a new dress that Maria had made for her. She demurely looked at her prayer book and gave the boys a glance that said volumes about how much more mature she thought she was than they. I smiled to myself.

Mass was magical, if one can say that about mass. There was a sense of something special in the air, and the candles augmented the feeling.

Alberto left quickly after mass, while the rest of the family stayed to exchange greetings with other people they knew.

"He has to put the gifts in the shoes before we get home." Erin whispered.

We made our way back home and Alberto nonchalantly joined us from across the street as we arrived.

The children rushed inside to see their shoes. Even Gabriela could not quite remain demure and mature in her excitement. After the loud exclamations were over, Maria invited the rest of us to sit in the living room while she got the food ready. Alberto served us an aperitif.

Maria soon called us in to eat. There were all kinds of food on the table, little pancakes and syrup, meat pies, sausages, three or four different kinds of bread, two different casserole dishes and a huge ham in the centre.

I had brought some red wine, and that was opened, as well as a bottle of white wine, which Gabriela was allowed to taste.

After the meal was over, Erin and I helped Maria clean up a bit in the kitchen and clear off the table. Then we went back to the living room to join the others.

I had placed some gifts on the coffee table earlier, when I had arrived, and now Maria came in, arms loaded with gifts which she placed on the table and around it.

Maria distributed the gifts to each child, one by one, and made them wait their turn to open them. "This way," she told me, "The suspense lasts a little longer, and gift-giving is not over in 10 seconds."

Each child received three gifts, a book, some clothes and a toy or game. Erin and Alberto each received two gifts and there was one for me as well. It was a stovetop espresso maker.

"I noticed you really like the stuff," Maria said, "and Erin told me you didn't have one."

"It's from both of us." Erin said.

"Thank you so much! I love it!" I exclaimed.

I saw that Maria had received a gift from Erin, but there were no others left on the table but those from myself. I got up to distribute them. I had got a serving platter for Maria and Alberto and a board game for the three children. There was also a travel coffee mug for Erin. I had noticed her eyeing mine on more than one occasion.

The children were sent to bed a few hours later, and the adults stayed up another hour until I finally yawned and declared that I should get going.

"I will accompany you." Alberto said. "You should not be walking alone that far at this time of night."

"I want to come too!" declared Erin.

"Alright." I said.

The three of us set off. The streets were mostly deserted. From time to time, one could hear the sound of revelers inside houses or on patios. Every once in awhile we would greet people still sitting in front of their houses.

As we came to Avenida San Martin, I happened to glance back and noticed a man walking behind us. Something about him looked familiar, but I could not place him.

I glanced back again, where the light was stronger and saw that the man was heading towards a doorway that lead to an apartment above one of the many boutiques. It was then that I recognized him.

He was the man I had seen a few months before, staring at me from his stool at a canteen, on my way home from Erin's place, the man who looked like he could be from the City.

"What's wrong?" Erin asked.

"Oh, nothing." I said. "I just thought I had seen someone I knew. It's no one I know though."

I put him out of my mind as we walked the rest of the way home through silent streets. I thanked Alberto and Erin for walking me home and went up to the silent apartment.

V

I slept quite late the next day, but finally got up when I started to hear noises in the kitchen. As I opened the door, I caught a whiff of coffee. I yawned and padded my way down to the kitchen.

It was not Leticia who was busy with the coffee pot. A man was in the kitchen. My heart jumped once and then I recognized him. With a shriek of joy I rushed at him and jumped into his arms.

For minutes I could do nothing but smile up at Asur. Then he bent down and kissed me.

"When did you get here?" I asked breathlessly. "How? Why?"

He grinned at me.

"I had some business in town, and decided to look up a few friends," he said. "I was already on the couch, sleeping when you came in. Luckily Felicia got home before you did, or I would have had to find a hotel."

"Or maybe a stable somewhere." I joked.

He kissed me on the nose. "Want some coffee?"

"Of course."

I sat at the table, drinking my coffee, drinking in the joy at having him so close to me.

We spent the day walking hand in hand around the city, especially the boardwalks along the shoreline.

"When do you have to leave again?" I asked him.

"Tomorrow."

My face fell. "But that's so soon."

"I know," he said gently, "But this is supposed to be a business trip only, remember?"

We had supper at home with Leticia. There were cakes and cookies that Leticia's mother had sent with her, and there were leftover sausages and pancakes that Maria had given me. We added a few vegetables and some rice and it made a good meal.

I passed the vegetables to Leticia and then served Asur.

"Thank you my princess," he said gallantly, and winked.

After supper, Asur and I sat outside on the balcony. Leticia had left again, to visit friends.

"Do you know why I love you so much?" I suddenly asked. "One of the reasons, I mean."

"Why?"

"Because I simply have so much fun with you." I said, "Because you enjoy so many of the same things that I enjoy. It's easy to imagine growing old with you and never being bored."

"This is something I appreciate as well," he said. "That and the passion you have for life itself, for anything that you put your mind to doing. You are such a passionate woman, Isabella."

"I think we share the same passions." I replied. "I think it is important for a couple to have a same purpose, a same cause."

"If we didn't, there would be a great void between us."

"Exactly."

I snuggled up to him and pulled his face down to mine. Instantly, I could feel the heat radiating from my chest, my heart was pumping like mad. I felt light-headed, as if I had had just a little too much to drink, and my skin was very sensitive to his touch.

"Asur," I said, pulling back, "how could I keep pushing you away before, when right now I feel like I could live permanently attached to you?"

Asur chuckled.

I looked over the edge of the balcony, across the shaded street, at the windows of the apartments in front of us.

"If we were still at my parents' home now," I said, "And sleeping in the chambre together, it would be impossible to resist you." I turned to him then, and traced my finger down the side of his cheek, "How did you manage to resist me then?"

"It wasn't always easy," He replied, "but I respect you more than anything, Isabella." Asur told me. "I would never want to hurt you."

He sat still for several minutes. "I read somewhere that sex is a spiritual thing. That God's plan for sex was for us to share not only in the act of creation, but also to create an intense bond, both spiritual and physical between spouses, comparing it even to Holy Communion, which is an intense meeting of God and man, both spiritual and physical."

"I wouldn't have had that if I had just taken advantage of you." Asur absently traced circles on the inside of my wrist with his thumb. It was his turn to stare across the street. Then he turned to look at me with his beautiful golden brown eyes. "When we make love, I want it to be complete; body and soul. I want you as a whole person. I don't just want to give you my body, I want to give you my soul too. Everything. It's what love is, you offer all you have, and you accept everything that is given."

I gasped slightly, eyes wide. His words gave me goosebumps.

"So while being with you in your parents' home was difficult for me," Asur continued, looking back across the street, "It was only difficult in the sense that it was all one way, not so much in the sense that I wanted you physically but had to restrain myself. I have never wanted something that was just physical. It wouldn't feel right to me, wouldn't appeal to me."

"Me neither." I declared.

"I know." Asur looked at me sideways, and the corner of his mouth turned up. "You are so passionate. You throw yourself into everything you do. Hard to imagine you not caring about the spiritual."

We sat in silence for awhile. By now the sun had gone down and the last of the colours in the sky were fading. A few birds called out here and there, and we could hear the occasional voices of people in the street below. A baby cried somewhere and then stopped.

I laid my head in the crook between his shoulder and his neck. His chin came around automatically to rest on my head, keeping my head in place. I breathed in his scent.

"I want it all." Asur murmured. "I want to follow God's plan for us. I want to be open to life, I want us to give and receive, not take. Love is a gift from God, it should be a religious experience, a prayer between the two of us, holy and pure. God made us both physical and spiritual. There must be balance between the two. If you live only for immediate physical gratification, then life becomes empty."

"Hmmmm." I agreed. "I do not understand a world which makes such a fuss over fleeting things. We are spiritual as well as physical beings but we often forget the spiritual. The emptiness, that void inside us, it cannot be filled with physical things."

With my left hand, I traced patterns up and down Asur's right arm. "On one hand, I am a physical being. I take pleasure in simple things, coffee that tastes just right, raindrops on my nose, the sound of waves crashing on the beach, the feel of sand between my toes, the way you smell." I smiled at him coyly. "On the other hand I am a spiritual being. I need spirit to spirit contact; long talks with close friends, philosophy, a song whose lyrics mean something, a poem, a conversation with God."

"Exactly!" Asur exclaimed, "There is balance to be had. If you condemn physical pleasure and only value what is spiritual, you miss out on the beauty of life, yet a life filled with carnal pleasure alone is a very lonely, empty life indeed."

We sat together, out on the balcony, for a very long time that night. I was loathe to leave him, and he, me. We talked about many things, but towards the end, we mostly just sat, holding hands and enjoying each other's presence.

At one point, Asur got up to get some blankets to cover us, as the breeze was a little cool and the humid air made it worse.

Birds chirping awoke me and I realized that we had both finally fallen asleep in the chairs outdoors. My neck was a bit stiff and I rolled my head to take out the kinks.

Until then, Asur had been breathing softly beside me, but now his breathing changed and I knew he was about to wake up.

"Morning princess," he said, opening one eye.

"Good morning, Charming."

"Sleep well?" he asked me.

I laughed.

"Lets get some breakfast," he said.

"Let's go out for breakfast." I said.

"Alright," he said. "Take me to your favourite place."

We went inside to freshen up a bit and then left. I thought I'd take him to the Café Esperanza, which was still my favourite place to go.

We strolled arm in arm through deserted streets. Most people did not have to work today, and were still asleep or just getting up.

Café Esperanza was just opening and we were among the first customers. We ordered a coffee each and a pastry, which we took out to eat on the terrace.

About halfway through our coffee, I was delighted to see David arrive with his violin.

"Oh look Asur." I said, "There's the violinist I was telling you about. We're in for a treat."

We watched David take his violin out of his case and set up to play. David glanced our way, nodded and winked at me.

"He seems to know you." Asur remarked.

I grinned. "I was introduced to him and we've talked a couple of times." I said, "I really do like his music."

David set his violin under his chin and started a lively version of *The Twelve Days of Christmas*.

"He certainly does have talent." Asur agreed.

We continued drinking our coffee, and talking, and David swung into *Deck the Halls*, followed by something I did not recognize.

When he was done with that, he stopped a bit, looked up at us and asked, "Does anyone have a special request?"

"Do you know *O Holy Night?*" I asked him. He nodded.

"Come sing with me." I pleaded with Asur. I grabbed him by the hand and led him to stand next to David, as the first strains of my favourite Christmas hymn floated out into the morning air.

O holy night, the stars are brightly shining;
It is the night of our dear Saviour's birth!
Long lay the world in sin and error pining,
'Til He appeared and the soul felt it's worth.
A thrill of hope, the weary soul rejoices,
For yonder breaks a new and glorious morn.

Asur's rich baritone blended perfectly with my alto. David nodded as he played, enjoying the singing as much as we. He joined us for the refrain.

Fall on your knees, O hear the angel voices!
O night divine, O night when Christ was born!
O night, O holy night, O night divine!
Fall on your knees, O hear the angel voices!
O night divine, O night when Christ was born!
O night divine, O night, O holy night!

When we had sung the whole hymn, David ended with a bit of a flourish and it was when there was a sudden, enthusiastic burst of applause that we noticed that a little crowd had stopped to listen.

"We should get together more often." David said. "We would be a real success."

"Unfortunately I'm only here on business and I'm leaving today." Asur replied with a smile.

"David, this is my friend Asur." I introduced them.

"More than just a friend, I think Rosa." David winked at me.

"Is it that obvious?" I asked, smiling in Asur's direction.

"Your faces light up when you look at each other." David lifted his violin up to his chin again.

"This one is for you two," he said.

The music that poured off the strings of his violin was soft, sweet and high. It was melancholy, and then it was calling, it was light and happy, then deep and sad.

"I wrote that for a very special girl I once new," he said when he had finished.

I was awestruck. "You wrote that?" I exclaimed. "You are really good! It is so beautiful!"

"My inspiration was more beautiful still." David replied, and started to play again, Christmas music that I recognized.

Before leaving, Asur and I stopped to put coins in David's violin case. He nodded his thanks and kept on playing. The notes of his music followed us on the breeze as we walked away.

VI

I was back in the Morales' home a week later, sitting on the front porch with Erin, sipping iced green tea and enjoying the last of our time off before a new semester started up.

Maria came outside with her own glass of iced green tea, and sat down on the steps in front of us.

"I see you put my gift to good use." I remarked, referring to the platter I had seen on the kitchen table earlier, full of fresh fruit.

"Yes" Maria smiled, "Thank you." She looked more tired than usual.

"Are you alright?" I asked her.

"Yes," she said, "Just a little tired from late nights and early mornings."

"So, did you get anything interesting for Christmas besides what Erin and I gave you?" I asked.

"Not really." Maria said. "There was a good book I wanted to read, that my mother bought for me."

"What about from Alberto?" I asked, wondering if Alberto had given her a present in private.

Maria and Erin looked at each other a moment before Maria hesitantly replied, "I haven't had a Christmas gift from Alberto in years."

I was shocked. "You haven't?"

Maria sighed. "I told you before that Alberto is um, very practical and not very expressive?"

"Yes, but…"

"I think personally he just doesn't like to shop and doesn't know what to get anyway." Maria said. "He once told me he didn't care if he got gifts anyway, and that it wasn't important to him. I think he thought that explained it and that it wouldn't make a difference to me either."

"But it does?" I asked.

"I can't help it if he grew up in a home where gift-giving wasn't a big deal." Maria said, "I personally grew up in a household where you didn't have to give big gifts, but making a person feel special and loved was a big deal. I understand that it might be unimportant to him, but I still can't seem to stop feeling a little disappointed every Christmas, or at my birthday."

"Well, and you have a right to be disappointed too." Erin replied.

"That may be, but I can't dwell on it, or I'll just be bitter." Maria replied. "Although I have to admit that some days it would be easier to give in to self-pity."

She smiled at Erin and I, "But at least I have you to thank for gifts."

"Maria, I'm going to be impolite, but I have to ask you anyway, why did you marry Alberto in the first place?" I asked. "I mean, has he always been like that? Didn't that bother you?"

"I knew he wasn't very demonstrative." Maria replied, "But he did show *some* affection back then. You know, I think if he would still show *some* affection now, I wouldn't mind so much about the gifts."

Maria sighed and stared at her empty glass of iced tea. "You know what girls, I'm going to tell you something, for when you have relationships of your own." She swirled her ice cubes around in the bottom of her glass. "If the man you are with is the right one you will know because he respects you and does not force you or try to coerce you into doing anything you feel is wrong." She stopped and looked at me.

"Erin already knows this, but Gabriela is Alberto's daughter by adoption. I already had her when we met. The man I was with, although I loved him deeply for many other reasons, did not think it was important to wait for marriage to have sex. He managed to get me to give in, I got pregnant, and that is when he disappeared."

"The bastard broke her heart." Erin muttered.

"Erin!" Maria exclaimed, "There is no need to swear!" To me, she said, "I have gotten over it."

She continued, "Number one, the man has to respect you and your beliefs. Number two, real affection is important. I don't mean affection that a man might use as a prelude to sex, I mean true affection, being happy with just holding hands, touching your shoulder when he talks to you, holding you around the waist, caressing your hair, just holding you and not expecting any more. Believe me, it makes a big difference later on, when sexual interest has diminished."

"Number three, you have to have fun with him. I don't mean he tells a joke and you laugh. I mean you are never bored together, you have most of the same interests, the same passions, the same tastes. You tease each other, you invent stories together or you sing together or whatever it is that you love to do together. You should be able to tell him anything. He has to be your best friend. When sexual attraction has worn off, it is the deep attraction you have for his person that keeps you together. Mental or spiritual orgasms are even better than the physical kind. Find a man like that and you will never wish to leave him."

The three of us were silent for a moment. I felt sorry for Maria, because in her words were the echo of sadness, the sadness of someone whose knowledge was gained too late.

"Are you ever lonely Maria?" I asked softly.

"Very often, Rosa." She replied, "And yet, I am never alone."

I sat down beside her on the steps and hugged her. Erin sat down on the other side of her and put her arms around her other side.

"You know," Maria said, her eyes a little misty, "I may often feel lonely, but there are times, like this moment, when I do not feel lonely at all."

We sat there, arms around each other for a long moment, while crickets chirped around us, and bees buzzed in the flowers of the trees surrounding the house. Every once in awhile a bird sang. For the longest time, there was no other sound, except for occasional noise from the street. Then loud argumentative voices broke through the relative silence.

Maria sighed. "I'd better go up," she said.

"Want to take a walk?" I asked Erin.

She stood up and stretched. "Okay"

We headed down the street and automatically turned towards Avenida San Martin.

Thunder rolled in the sky. I looked up. The sky was still blue. We still had some time before the storm. We arrived on Avenida San Martin and turned to walk in the direction of Café Esperanza.

The sun passed behind a cloud as we neared the café. I could see David playing the violin again.

Erin suddenly stopped in her tracks. I turned around and saw a look akin to horror on her face.

"What's wrong?" I asked

"I can't believe it! I don't believe it! That,…that's him!"

She scowled deeply. "Who?" I asked.

"That piece of scum," she muttered, "That's the guy who broke Maria's heart, the one who disappeared 12 years ago. He's back!"

"Where?"

"There!" she said, pointing straight at David. "Let me at him! I'll give him a piece of my mind!" She started stalking towards the musician.

"Wait!" I grabbed her arm. "Let's not make a scene alright? Wait until he's done."

David had seen us coming and evidently he recognized Erin and realized that the look of murder on her face was meant for him, because he finished his piece of music rather quickly, put his violin in his case, and came towards us.

He looked hesitantly from me to Erin, and back to me and I shrugged my shoulders. I couldn't help him.

"You scum!" Was what Erin said first. She glared at him. If eyes could kill, a thousand knives would have pierced him by now.

"I probably deserve that." He replied.

"Darn right you do!"

"I suppose it would not make a difference if I said I am sorry and I can explain?"

"It had better be a darn good explanation." Erin spat.

"I think Maria should hear it too." David said evenly.

"What makes you think she wants to?"

David sighed. "Can you take me to see her Erin?"

"She's married, and doesn't need you to come and wreck her life again."

"Erin," David was trying to stay calm, "I *know* that she is married. I do not *want* to wreck her life again. I only think that she deserves an explanation."

"Tell me why I should take you anywhere near my sister and open up her wounds again." Erin crossed her arms and tapped her foot impatiently on the ground.

I put a hand on her shoulder. "Don't you think we should at least hear his story before judging?" I murmured to her. To David I said, "That piece of music, the one you played for…my friend and I, your inspiration, that was Maria wasn't it?"

Erin must have heard the hesitation in my voice when I said that, for she turned around and looked at me, "Your…friend?" she asked suspiciously.

She turned and pointed a finger at David, "You," she said, "be quick with an explanation, and you," she said, pointing at me, "are going to tell me about your *friend* later."

David flashed a sudden grin at me and winked, while Erin's back was still turned, but by the time she had turned back to him, his face was perfectly serious again.

"You do remember that I left to work on a ship to make some money?" David asked Erin. "I left, but with the full intention of coming back. I did not just leave her like that. I knew about the baby, I wanted to make some money so we could be married. I could not do that on a musician's salary."

"So, why didn't you come back?" Erin's tone was still accusing.

"My contract was over, and we were heading home on the ship." David said. "Our ship hit a sudden tropical storm."

"A likely story." Snorted Erin.

Now David lost his patience. He grabbed her forearms with his two hands and looked into her eyes. "I said I had an explanation. I think it is an acceptable one. I do not care if you believe me or not. You may choose to keep your anger and chew upon it. All I want to do is be able to tell the truth to Maria. If she chooses to reject it as you do, then so be it. At least I will have tried. Now, may I continue please."

Erin's eyes opened wide and she nodded.

"We hit a reef. I fell and hit my head. Someone grabbed me and threw me in a lifeboat. We were lucky. The place we were wrecked in was a busy passage for boats. We were picked up the next day. I was still unconscious."

"I was in a coma for weeks," he said. "The people in the lifeboat I was with knew my first name, but none of them knew my last name nor where I was from exactly. The captain of our ship was in a different boat and was probably picked up by a different ship."

"When I came around, I remembered nothing. I could not even remember my own name. It took a long time for me to remember enough to contact my parents. By that time, she had just gotten married." He looked at Erin with some hurt in his face and said, "She did not wait very long for me, did she?"

"It had been four months already from the date you were supposed to come back when she met Alberto. She'd already had the baby. She'd had no news from you, so she accepted his invitation to go for supper. They got married eight months later." Erin said. "We did think it was a little fast, but they seemed so sure of themselves."

"If you do not mind." David said, I would like to meet Maria, before I tell the rest of my story."

"Alright." Erin sighed. "But you have to promise to do as I tell you. Stay outside, and I will go and get her and prepare her. Otherwise it'll be a huge shock."

"I agree to that."

The three of us turned towards Maria and Alberto's home, each one of us silent, lost in our thoughts.

When we had arrived, I stayed out on the veranda with David, while Erin went in to talk to Maria. I could hear their voices, but could not make out what they were saying. Then I heard Ian's voice loud and clear, "Mama, que te pasa? What's wrong?"

I got up and said, "I think I'll go get the children."

I arrived in the kitchen in time to hear Maria tell Erin, "I can't go out there!"

"You have to." Erin said. "But we'll be with you, right Rosa?"

"I'm going to send Gabriela with the boys to get some ice-cream down the street." I replied, going up the stairs.

"It'll ruin their dinner." Said Maria.

"It'll keep them out of our hair for awhile."

"Ice-cream!" Yelled Ian.

"Ice-cream!" answered Roberto from the top of the stairs. He came rushing down the stairs, bounding past me as I walked up to get Gabriela.

The door to her room was open, and she was sitting on her bed, listening to music.

"Hi." I said. "Can you do me a favour?"

"What?" she asked, sitting up straighter.

"I need to do something with your mom, but the boys are a little wild, and I thought,..." A sudden idea came to my mind, "Since it is the feast of the Holy Family today, I want to treat you to some ice-cream from that ice-cream place down the street. Do you think you could take the boys?"

"Ok" she said, smiling. "Is it really the feast-day of the Holy Family today, Rosa?"

"It certainly is." I said.

I ushered the three children out the side door, gave Gabriela some money at the gate and waved goodbye. I turned and saw David staring at them from the reasonably well-concealed front veranda.

I walked back towards him.

"That is my daughter," he said.

"Yes."

"She is beautiful. Like her mother."

"Yes."

"It seems her mother does not want to see me," he said sadly.

"It has been a shock." I replied. "I think she is only afraid to see you." I stepped back inside.

In the kitchen, Maria did not look afraid, she looked positively petrified.

"He's not a monster, you know." I said, "He won't hurt you."

"I know." Maria said. "It is not him that I am afraid of. I am afraid of myself."

She suddenly pulled herself up straight. "Let's do this then," she said, "Before the children come back."

I led the way to the front veranda. Erin followed, holding Maria's hand.

David stood up as we came outside. For a minute, no one spoke. Maria and David stared at each other, as if trying to decide what to say or do next. Finally, "Sit down." Maria invited.

David sat down again.

Maria sat down on the chair furthest from him. Erin sat down beside her. I sat on the steps.

"Erin has told you my story, I imagine." David said softly.

Maria nodded. "You were in a coma and lost your memory," she said.

David nodded. "We were sailing in the South Sea."

"So far away?" Maria asked, "You were only supposed to go around the continent."

"Yes," David replied, "But my Captain was solicited at the last minute to go further. I didn't have time to send a message before we left and by the time I was free we were no longer connected to the net. It took us over four weeks to get there, and then I had the accident before I had a chance to send a message from there. A bad storm blew in and we lost the ship. When we were rescued, we were taken to the nearest coastal village. From there, I was transported to a larger town and put into a hospital."

"That is where I woke up. I had no idea how I had gotten there, nor who I was. The crew member that had brought me there was gone. He had told the doctors that I had been a crewman on the *Flor* and that my name was David. That was all he knew. And for a long time, that was all I knew."

"My memory started to come back in flashes. I would remember doing things with people, but I had no idea who they were. I would remember fishing with my father, but I could not remember his name. Then I remembered saying goodbye to you Maria, just before my ship sailed."

David looked at Maria for a minute. "That was the worst. I could see your face, I knew you were someone special, I knew I had to get back to you, but I could not remember your name, nor even where you lived."

"Eventually, your first name came to me, and about the same time, I could remember my last name, where I came from and my parents' names. The hospice I stayed at contacted my parents, who came as soon as they could to see me and bring me home. But when I asked them about you, they knew nothing."

"We sailed home, not long after, and…"

"Wait a minute." I said. I looked from Maria, to David to Erin. "There's something I don't understand. Am I missing something? David's parents knew nothing about Maria?"

Maria smiled. "David is not from San Isidor," she said.

"I come from a small village up the coast." David told me. "A small fishing village, not far from Pueblito. At the time, I was young, I was doing my own thing, and I did not communicate much with my parents. I did not tell them much about what was going on in my life. I only told them before I left on the ship that I had a girlfriend and that I wanted to marry her, but I had only mentioned her first name."

"They figured that Maria lived in San Isidor, because that is where I was at the time I left, but San Isidor is huge, and she could also have come from any one of the small towns and villages surrounding it."

"We went home to San José, our village, where my mother fattened me up again, and I worked on trying to remember things."

"I contacted the captain of the *Flor* to see if I had told him anything about you, but he knew very little. He put me in touch with a few of the sailors I had spent more time with, and they were a bit more helpful, but only a bit." He smiled with irony, "I now knew your last name was either O'Hara, or O'Dea or one of those Celtic names. I couldn't very well call up everyone whose name was O-something in the San Isidor area."

"I decided to come back to San Isidor to see if that would trigger more memories."

"I met someone in the street who recognized me. You remember John Malley?"

Maria nodded.

"He stopped me in the street, as I walked by. 'You don't say hi to friends anymore?' he asked me. 'I'm sorry.' I replied, 'Your face looks familiar, but I had an accident and lost a bit of my memory, including a lot of names.'"

"He told me his name and we got to talking. I asked him about you and that is when he told me you had just gotten married."

"I'm sorry." Maria said, a little hoarsely.

"The news hit me like a brick in the chest. I had to sit down for a minute. I couldn't believe my ears."

David fell silent.

Erin cleared her throat. "Um," she said, looking at both Maria and David, then at me. "Maybe we should leave you two alone to talk a bit out here."

I nodded. "We'll be in the kitchen if you need us." I told Maria.

The two of us got up and walked towards the front door, as behind us, David walked over to sit in the chair next to Maria.

VII

Classes had started up again. I had 2 more classes with Erin this semester, but none that required any teamwork. We still met regularly to do homework together and look up cases to study though.

On one such occasion, I arrived at the Morales' home before Erin.

Maria greeted me in the kitchen, and offered me a glass of orange juice.

"How are you doing?" I asked.

Maria narrowed her eyes as she looked at me. "Do you want a polite answer, or do you want the real answer?" she asked.

"Honestly? I want the truth." I said.

"Honestly," she said, "I've got a really bad case of the regrets."

I sat down at the table. "You're talking about David."

She sat down across from me. "Uh-huh."

I was silent.

"You know, if I had just waited a few more months…" She said, "I could be married to a passionate, sensitive, talented person."

She looked at me with sadness in her eyes. "Alberto is a good person," she said. "A very good person. But he is a very practical person. Which I am not. I need something more. I need to think about things, I need to express ideas, there is this whole part of me that he does not know and never will because he cannot understand it. He does not understand dreams. They are too abstract. He has never wanted more than a good job, a home and a family."

"You know, David went into a bit of a depression after he found out I had married."

"He did?" I was surprised.

"He took it rather hard, apparently." Maria sighed. "I feel so bad sometimes. To think, Gabriela could have grown up knowing her father."

"There must be a reason." Maria continued. "I cannot believe that there is no reason for this. If only to make it easier to bear, I have to believe that there is a reason that this is all happening."

"God's ways *are* mysterious." I said. "I...lost someone I loved very much once." I hesitated, not knowing how much I should say.

"In the end, it permitted me to...see other people in a different light."

"I keep thinking, perhaps there is a reason why we have found each other again." Maria said. "Perhaps later, it will all make sense. Even if it is only to have some kind of absolution, things put right between us, and then left behind. It helps to think that."

"Hope," I said. "Hope keeps us alive. Hope keeps us sane."

"It's the only thing keeping me going right now." She sighed, "It's hard now, but I know this will pass. It is almost as if someone I loved had died. I mourn what could have been. Eventually, I *will* get over it."

****

I was kept busy for weeks after that. Mid-terms came and went. Spring was in the air. The scent of blossoms on the trees drifted my way as I studied in my room in the evenings. I started using the ceiling fan again.

I saw the same man I thought came from the City again twice, but thought nothing more of it. Both times he was sitting outside at a café on Avenida San Martin.

I had not had any more opportunities to talk to Maria alone, as the children or Alberto were always around when I was there, but I knew through Erin that she had not seen David again in person, but did correspond with him from time to time through the com system.

The Lenten season was drawing to a close. I went to Passion Sunday mass with Erin, Maria and the family. Passion Sunday was a big feast in San Isidor. The whole thing started off with a procession from a little chapel a few blocks away from the Cathedral. People lined the streets, waving branches and an altar boy, carrying a monstrance and in it a consecrated host, started off the procession. Following him was a priest on a donkey, representing Jesus, and behind, various deacons and lay people followed, representing the disciples and Jesus' close followers, including Mary his mother and Mary Magdalene.

Different choirs from different parishes stood on street corners, singing hymns, and the crowd joined in. When the procession passed, the people on the sidelines joined in, so by the time the procession reached the Cathedral, a throng of people followed behind, singing and dancing.

There were too many people to all fit into the Cathedral, so a large com system was set up outside to permit people to follow along.

When mass was over, we paraded home with our blessed palm branches. We were going to make special bread for Easter.

There was a lot of laughter in the kitchen as Maria got out bowls and the children chattered excitedly. Erin found the ingredients and I divided up utensils between the children.

Alberto went outside to do some jobs in the yard.

The children were happily mixing flour and baking soda and cheese and onions and milk and other things, and we were supervising, trying to keep the mess down to a minimum.

"It would be sooo much easier to just do it myself." Maria said with a smile. "But look at how much fun they are having."

"Too bad they aren't so enthusiastic when the time comes to clean up." Remarked Erin.

When the dough was ready, we started shaping it into special forms. This was the part that the children liked best. Gabriela especially, took pains on the details.

"You do this every Easter?" I asked Maria.

"My mother used to do this with us." She replied, "It's traditional around here, although not everyone does it anymore. I've been doing since Gabriela was about three."

While the freshly baked bread was cooling off, the three of us cleaned up the kitchen with much laughter. Gabriela helped for a bit, then went outside to join her brothers and father in the yard.

"You seem to be feeling better." I remarked to Maria, after a bit.

She regarded me intently, with the same green eyes as her sister.

"It's amazing really, how we humans can continue to live life as if nothing were wrong." She replied, "How we can walk around and do ordinary things as if we weren't torn up inside, as if we weren't regretting all the little mistakes and wrong decisions that lead us to places we don't want to be anymore, but are not free to leave."

She sighed, "I feel like I am two people. On one level, I laugh and joke and have fun. I go around the house doing all the same things I always do. Nothing seems to have changed. But deep inside, I feel so empty. I can forget for awhile, push it away, but the feeling is always there."

Erin and I were silent for a while, wiping dishes and putting them away.

"Human capacity, human strength is amazing." I said finally, "I am always amazed at the ability we have, to do what is right, to search for the truth, to put others first, to sacrifice ourselves, to get up from a fall and to keep walking."

"I know people who have suffered, not emotionally necessarily, but from oppression and poverty, and they get together and beautiful things happen. From practically nothing, they are able to build something, where each of them is responsible and everyone gets an equal share. Their experience has toughened them and taught them something."

"Sometimes," Erin said softly, "happiness comes through doors you didn't know you left open." She smiled, "Saw that written somewhere, once."

"I have to believe that." Maria said, "I want to believe that there is a reason for the way things turned out in my life, that God has a plan for me, that He wants to use me in some way. If I am here, in this particular place, in this particular situation, it is because it is God's will, whatever that is. If I do not believe this, I don't think I can accept how things turned out in my life. I just don't think I can handle it."

"Have faith, and hope." Erin said.

"But it is so hard to keep hoping. It is hard to keep on going like everything is the same. It is hard to keep on loving and caring, hard to be cheerful. Well, maybe not all that hard, but it is hard to not be thinking of how I would like my life to be, instead."

Maria sighed, "I know there are ups and downs in life, but why does it feel like there are never any ups in mine? I am either at sea level or down in a valley, but there are no mountains in my life." She spread out her arms and twirled in the kitchen, "I feel like scaling a mountain. I want to dance in an alpine meadow, I want to feel the wind blowing hard on my face." She smiled, "I want to discover the tiny stunted flowers."

"I'm with you!" I said heartily, "When do we leave for the mountains?"

"Don't forget me behind!" grinned Erin.

VIII

Easter came and went, then came the rush of studying for final exams and finishing essays and projects. I had decided to take a break in the summer, so I applied for a few summer jobs for students in social services that were posted in the lobby reserved for students in Social Services at the University.

I also applied to work part-time at Café Esperanza.

The jobs in Social Services went to other students, but thanks to the fact that many of the people already working at the café knew me at least by sight, including the owner, I got a part-time job there. I did not need more than that anyway, as my parents were regularly transferring money to my bank account to pay for my daily needs. My room was taken care of by the Government branch of Criminal Justice that takes care of Witness Protection, for as long as I would be studying. I only had to pay for my food and other necessities.

I wanted to work, to feel like I was contributing, at least a little bit, to my own cause. I also did not want to be sitting around all summer with nothing to do. I wanted to be around people, doing something useful, at least part of the time.

Working at Café Esperanza turned out to be even better than the Social Services jobs would have been. When things were slow, I often talked to the other servers and some of the regular clients.

It happened every once in awhile that someone would have a problem that I was able to help them out with, or at least refer them to an organization that could help them. This was much better than sitting in an office all day, filing things, which is what the lucky students who got the social service jobs were doing.

David still came regularly to play the violin, and I talked to him when I had time.

The summer months passed quickly. My time off was often spent with Erin, Maria and the children. They took me to the beach, where I had my first taste of swimming. The children dove and glided through the water like dolphins and laughed at my attempts to paddle around like a dog.

I enjoyed walking bare feet on the fine sand of the beach. It was soft, wet and cool when you dug your feet into it, unlike the coarse, burning hot sand of the City, which was always full of pebbles.

One weekend, Alberto took the children camping in the mountains an hour or two from San Isidor, and Erin and I helped Maria to clean the house from top to bottom and go through things. Anything that was too small, or rarely used was taken to charity, and used or broken things were thrown out. A lot of papers were put in the recycling, those that had nothing on the back, Maria put in a box so the children could draw on them.

On the Sunday evening, when all was done, and we were waiting for the others to arrive, we sat, with our feet in the air, sipping pina coladas.

"Ahhhhh," sighed Maria, contentedly, "Cleaning house is almost as therapeutic as cleaning your soul."

****

In September my second year of studies in social services started. I kept my job at the Café Esperanza, but reduced the number of hours I worked a week. When I wasn't behind the counter, serving up espressos, lattes and cappuccinos as well as regular coffee, I was often sitting at one of the outside tables, doing research, writing up papers or communicating with other people on my PCD. I had a headset which, when I wasn't using it to talk to another person on their com system, I used to listen to music files stored in my PCD.

When David or some other musician came to play, I would turn off the music on my PCD and listen to them play instead.

One day, as I was ending my shift behind the counter, David walked in with a guitar and invited me to sit with him in a secluded area of the café with him.

"I want to show you something," he said.

He slipped me a piece of paper, on which I could see musical notes and lyrics.

"Do you think you could sing that if I played it for you?" David asked.

"I don't think it would be too hard." I smiled. "I can read music. I played the piano regularly when I was with my parents. Play it for me please."

He moved his chair back to make more room, and softly, began to play. Reading the notes, I hummed along softly. It wasn't too hard to follow.

"Shall we try it?" I asked.

I sang the first two verses, and then the chorus:

You are the road I travel
You are the miracle I unravel
For every step I tread,
Another blessing is shed.
Unexpected, amazing
I cannot look back, to you I cling
Down the road, I will go
It beckons, I must follow.

There were two more verses afterwards, which I also sang. "You wrote this?" I asked him.

He nodded. "A long time ago," he said. "I have been working on it recently, I changed some of the words and some of the music."

"I like it." I said.

"I'd like you to sing it with me sometimes at the café. If you would like."

"I'd love to." I replied.

So it was, I started to sing with David every once in awhile, after my shifts. I enjoyed singing, it often lifted my spirits, when I was feeling especially homesick.

****

The months of September, October and November rolled quickly by. It was early December, and Maria was in her kitchen, putting the finishing touches on her Advent wreath as I walked in with books, notes and my PCD.

"Oh!" I said, "That's pretty! You are always so good with your hands. I can draw a decent picture, and I can follow a pattern, but you have real talent. I wish I could do things like that."

"I wish I could sing like you do." Maria replied, "I can carry a tune, but I've heard you sing, in Church, and I don't compare. David tells me you sing with him at the Café from time to time."

"Speaking of David, have you seen him again?" I asked.

"No," Maria replied, "I prefer not to see him, we communicate through the com system, when we chat."

She got up and went to the fridge. I'm going to have myself a glass of juice," she said, "Want some?"

"All right, thank you."

I left my books on the table in the kitchen and went to see what the children were doing in the living room. I could hear them giggling through the door.

I stepped through the door.

"Whoa!" I gasped.

The living room had been repainted in a vibrant deep burgundy red with cream accents and a new library lined one wall which now held a lot of the books and games that used to spill out of a much smaller, older one. The chairs and coffee table had been rearranged to open up the space there.

I turned back to the kitchen. "When did you have time to do this?" I asked.

"Oh, it didn't take too long." Maria said. "I did it last weekend when Alberto and the boys went fishing on Alberto's father's boat. I'd been planning on doing it for a long time, and I finally got fed up with the mess in here."

"The funny thing is, Alberto never noticed anything until two days after he came home." Maria told me.

"Really?" I said.

Maria laughed. "Really. But let me tell you the funniest thing. He suddenly came into the kitchen and asked me 'What did you do to the living room?!'"

Maria proceeded to tell the story. She had laughed, then told him that she had painted it the previous weekend.

"Well," he had said, on the defensive now, "I got in really late the last two nights and went straight to bed."

Maria had then reminded Alberto that the light was on when he went through there to go up the stairs to bed.

He had replied, a bit irritably, that he wasn't looking at anything but the stairs when he went up. Maria happened to be wiping dishes while they had been talking, and some were waiting to be put away, so she had asked him, jokingly, if they were going to put themselves away. Which is often the way, Maria told me, that Alberto asks her to do things, when he thinks they obviously need doing. At that, he had stalked off.

"For the next five or ten minutes, he wouldn't talk to me." Maria said. "I thought to myself, oops, maybe I should not have asked him quite like that. Not only that, but what we had for supper wasn't his favourite. So I thought maybe he was in a bad mood over that."

"I suddenly wondered if he had actually liked the way the living room was now. So I decided to ask him later, once he wasn't mad anymore."

Maria had started to get a bit impatient and finally asked him, why he was so upset. Was it because of the way she had asked him to put the dishes away or because they had only had soup for supper and no meat?

"No" he had replied, pouting. "I give you a compliment and all you can do is criticize me!"

"What!" My jaw dropped. Maria laughed, a deep throaty laugh.

"I'm sure my face looked just like yours when I said the same thing," she said, still laughing. "He repeated what I had said."

Her voice became high-pitched and tinny, "I painted it *last* weekend."

Maria had replaced her jaw to normal position and exclaimed, "That was a compliment? *What* did you do to the living room?"

"Oh yeah," he had exclaimed sarcastically, "I said it like that!"

"I may have exaggerated the tone of voice a bit, but not by much." Maria told me. "I told him I didn't even know if he had liked it or not. I could tell he was tuning me out. He does that as soon as there is any conflict. 'That was not a compliment,' I tried to tell him. 'That was a question. A question isn't a compliment.' He didn't answer back."

"Unbelievable!" I chuckled.

"I still shake my head." Maria said, shaking her head. "You know what, it just goes to show that maybe we should always just take everything as a compliment, even when it isn't one. I bet the world would be a happier place if we all did that."

"I bet you are right." I said. "I think I may try that out. I have a belligerent professor at the university that I can try that out with right away."

Maria's laughter pealed out once again and I joined in.

IX

When the final exams for the fall semester were finished, Maria and Erin invited me to spend the Christmas Holidays with them again. Erin offered to share her room with me and Maria set up a folding bed in there.

It was December 22, and the whole house was full of the smells of baking and of evergreen boughs.

Just as I was getting ready to go to bed, I received a text message from Leticia.

Just received a message from your brother, Leo. He says to be careful, do not walk around alone anymore, it seems some old friends have followed you.

I no longer felt sleepy after reading that, so after lying in bed for an hour, I slipped on a light housecoat over my nightshirt and went quietly down the stairs to the living room.

There was a lamp on in the living room and Maria was sitting in one of the armchairs, holding a mug of something that looked like slightly yellow milk.

"Can't sleep again tonight," she said, "I am a prisoner of my own thoughts."

"Then we are two prisoners."

"Want some warm chamomile milk? It helps me sometimes." She offered.

I accepted and we went to the kitchen where she warmed milk in a pan, then added chamomile and honey and poured it into a mug for me.

"What was keeping you up?" I asked her.

"Oh, the same things that always keep me up." She sighed, "You know, once, when our Mother Mary appeared to Saint Bernadette

Soubirous she told her 'I do not promise to bring happiness for you in this world, but in the next.'"

"I've been reading the lives of a few saints and it seems to me that not very many of them had very happy lives. Most saints seem to suffer a lot, and unlike me, they endure it patiently of course. So I guess if I am ready to give up my happiness that would be putting myself on the path to sainthood? Not that I am anywhere near sainthood. Just that this seems to be a requirement for sainthood."

"I think you are probably closer to sainthood than I am." I replied, "You are so much more patient than I am."

"Not always." Maria smiled. "You know, I always thought that God wished us to be happy, even here on earth. I thought we just had to follow his laws, do the right thing, and then we would be happy. But I think I was wrong, not that he doesn't want us to be happy, but happiness doesn't always happen, sometimes you have to suffer too."

"I am being silly," Maria shook her head, "I think I am suffering, when actually so many people suffer much more than I. Jesus suffered much more than I. How can I really think I am suffering?"

"Enough about me, what were you thinking about." Maria asked, "If I'm not prying too much. You don't often talk about yourself, perhaps you prefer not to?"

"There is a reason that I do not talk much about myself." I said. "I think someday soon I will tell you why and you will understand, but until then, I cannot say much. I will tell you this, I received a message today that I should no longer walk alone in the city, that certain people who want to harm me may know where I am."

Maria was silent.

"I have probably already said too much." I said. "I think maybe, I should go back to my own apartment and not put you in any danger too."

"Do you really think that is necessary?" Maria asked.

"Well, I doubt anything would happen, but just in case, I wouldn't want you or the children to be in danger too. I think I would be safer at my apartment too."

"By yourself?"

"No, with Leticia."

"With Leticia?"

I sighed, "Yeah, she's um, able to help me if I need help."

****

The morning sun was shining through the windows in Maria's kitchen as I sat at the counter, eating breakfast. Erin sat at the other end, and Maria was taking bites here and there, standing up at the stove.

"Alberto will walk you back to your apartment." Maria told me.

"Oh," I said, "I don't think that's necessary, for now."

"Did you not get a message telling you not to go alone?" Maria asked.

"Well yes, but I think I'll be okay just this once. I don't want you going out of your way for me."

"Alberto will accompany you." Maria said firmly, "I will feel better if he does."

"All right." I sighed.

"I'd go too, but I have an appointment today." Erin told me.

"That's all right." I replied.

We left the house, with the two boys yelling goodbye at us and Gabriela smiling and waving. The birds were not yet quiet, although the early morning chatter had diminished. We met a few people hurrying to do last minute errands before Christmas.

Avenida San Martin was busy, but the little streets we turned onto to head towards my apartment were almost deserted.

Alberto did not talk very much, so I admired the Christmas decorations people had put outside their homes along the way.

As I turned to admire a particularly pretty bow, I caught sight of a familiar looking figure, who promptly disappeared around the corner. I stopped, perplexed.

"What's wrong?" Alberto wanted to know.

I thought I saw…my brother." I replied. I shook my head, it must have just been someone who looked a lot like Leo Martin.

"You have a brother?" Alberto raised his eyebrow. "You never said."

"It just never came up, I guess." I hoped my cheeks were not going too red. "We don't see a lot of each other."

"There is more to you than what we see, I think." Alberto said.

"Isn't there always?" I asked, "More to people than we think?"

"Some people hide more than others." Alberto said.

We kept on walking for a couple of minutes, and suddenly I heard footsteps moving quickly towards us from behind. Instinctively, I turned around, and gasped.

The man I had seen a few times previously, who I thought might come from the City, was coming towards us. The look on his face was not reassuring.

"Who's that?" Alberto asked.

"I don't know," I replied, "but something tells me we should run."

We took off to the left, as we were at a street corner. As soon as we started running, the man behind us started to run as well. I could hear his feet pounding behind us.

"We have to find a shop that's open." Alberto gasped.

"This way!" I replied, and swung to the right at the next street corner. I knew where there was a convenience store not far.

I was starting to get tired, I am not a runner nor am I even close to being an accomplished athlete. Adrenaline was keeping me going, but I knew I was slowing down. The man behind us was getting closer.

I could see the corner store now, and that gave me a burst of energy. If only we could make it there to get help. We dashed up the sidewalk, just as two men came out of the doorway. I slid to a sudden halt, grabbing Alberto's arm.

"Oh nooooo!" I moaned in desperation. "Not him!"

I suddenly knew who exactly it was that had orchestrated the attempt on my life, and who was most likely also responsible for the death of Ben. He was standing right there in front of me, on the doorstep of the corner store, smirking at me.

It was Garrick Sanche, the same boy who had bullied Asur, grown up now, working for his father's business, which was one of the most notorious in its flagrant disrespect for the dignity and rights of its workers.

"We have to get out of here." I said desperately.

"Through that gate!" Alberto grabbed my hand and ran. We made it through the gate of a private house, and Alberto slammed the gate behind us and locked it. We ran to the back of the yard, which was deserted. Alberto gave me a hand up, and I flipped over the fence, into the neighbour's yard. There, an elderly lady gaped at me in surprise.

"¡Entra en la casa y llama a la policía!" I yelled at her, as Alberto pulled himself over the fence behind me. He, in turn told the lady to get inside, and call the police to say two people were being pursued by criminals.

I could hear a commotion in the other yard. "Over the fence!" I heard someone yell as we ran out the front gate and turned right down the street.

"Got to go back." Puffed Alberto. "Make them think we went on. They won't expect us to turn back."

Two doors down, we ran through another gate, into another deserted backyard. We ran to the back right-hand corner and hopped the fence to the diagonal neighbour.

One of them must have caught a glimpse of us, because I heard a shout. "There they are!"

Alberto swore under his breath.

I was getting really tired. I just was not going to be able to keep running. "We need a place to hide." I said.

"Come!" Alberto said. "Bend over, so they don't see you." He led me to the shed in the back.

"Please God, let it be open," he said.

It was. We quietly got in and closed the door. "Is there a lock on it?" I whispered. Alberto checked.

"I think it only locks from the outside." He whispered."

"Can't we shove something into the handles to lock it?" I asked.

"There!" he said, grabbing an old broom and shoving it through the two handles of the doors.

"All we have to do is keep quiet." Alberto said.

In that instant, I heard them crashing over the fence. "Which way did they go?" One asked.

"I don't know you idiot, weren't you watching?" Someone else replied.

"Quiet you two! Stop your bickering!" a third voice came, which, I was certain, belonged to Garrick.

"They can't have gotten far." Said one of the voices, the first, or was it the second? I couldn't tell.

"Check down the street." Garrick said. His voice came from the other side of the door to the shed. I did not dare breathe. The doors rattled, as he tried to pull them open.

"No one here," he said. "It's locked."

I almost fainted in relief. I could hear their voices fading in the distance.

"How long do we wait?" I asked.

"I don't know." Alberto whispered back.

I don't know how much time passed. Hours? Minutes? I was so on edge that the passing of time seemed like a dream, a lifetime within a few minutes.

Finally, Alberto said, "I think we can leave now." I haven't heard anything in a long time."

"Ok." I nodded.

Cautiously, he slid the broom out of the handles, opened the door a crack., and peered outside. "I see nothing out there," he said. Slowly, we made our way out of the shed, and looked carefully about. Still seeing nothing, we started to make our way towards the front of the house. As we did so, I heard movement behind us.

I turned around to see the man from the City blocking our way back to the shed. He was grinning.

"Good day Isabella." I heard Garrick's voice from behind me. "I figured if we waited long enough you would come out of there." I turned to see him blocking the way to the front. Two more men came to circle us.

"Isabella?" Alberto looked at me questioningly.

The bigger of the two men grabbed Alberto.

"Get rid of him." Garrick said.

"Nooooo!" I yelled.

Alberto struggled to get free, as the man unsheathed a knife. I kicked him as hard as I could, aiming for right between the legs, but missed and caught his inner thigh instead. The man yelled, and lunged at Alberto. Alberto fell to the ground. There was a sudden commotion as five or six other people came running into the back yard.

Then pain seared into my back. I was falling. I could not stand anymore, the pain was too great. I could not seem to breathe properly anymore. My head swam. There was nothing left but pain, and then, blessedly, there was no more pain.

Book Three

I

All was black for a few moments, then the light came back. I seemed to be floating. I saw Asur running to me. Leo Martin and four or five others were busy dealing with Garrick and his men. I could see my body lying in the grass, not far from Alberto's body.

I suddenly wondered what my parents would think of my death, and instantly, I was with them in the dining room of the manor. Tessie was sitting at the table, eating with them.

My mother sat up suddenly and gasped. "Something has happened to Isabella!" She said. "I can feel it!"

"Come, come now dear." Said my father. "That's silly. You can't just feel things like that."

"No, really." My mother said, "I can feel it. I feel her! Get Asur on the line please!"

Looking at my mother's face, my father decided that it would be best to get Asur on the com system instead of arguing.

"Mother! I'm here!" I tried to say, but I seemed to only be able to scream in my mind.

My father tried repeatedly to get a hold of Asur, but Asur was not answering.

"I just know something is wrong!" My mother moaned.

I moved closer to my mother, wanting to comfort her. She shivered slightly. Tessie came to her and hugged her.

I suddenly thought of my friends who worked so hard for social justice, Karl, Fatima and Alex, Ismael, Dominique and Emile. In the instant I thought of each one, it seemed for a moment I was right there with them.

I vaguely saw my childhood friend Alisha and then thought of Aunt Isobel.

Aunt Isobel was in her kitchen, talking with her cook about what preparations to make for the evening meal. She shivered slightly and turned around.

"What's wrong?" asked the cook.

"I don't know, I just get the feeling someone else is here." She answered, looking around.

I did not try to say anything, I knew she would not hear me anyway.

At that moment, the com system rang. It was my mother.

"Isobel." My mother sounded distraught. "Something's wrong, I can feel it!"

"Calm down, Elizabeth." Aunt Isobel said. "What is wrong?"

"I have this horrible feeling that something has happened to Isabella." My mother said. "And now we can't get a hold of Asur. It felt like she was in the room with us, just minutes ago, and now I have a really bad feeling."

I drifted away. I was getting the hang of the drifting. I only had to think of going somewhere to be there. I drifted aimlessly through the streets of the City. In reality, it lasted perhaps seconds, but for me, there seemed to be no time. Or time seemed to have slowed down. Or perhaps, I was in all of time.

I went back to the time I first talked to Ben, outside my parents' home. I saw the employee who'd been caught stealing walk away, I saw myself walk up the path, and heard our conversation.

I drifted forward in time and saw myself with Asur, with my parents and my friends.

My thoughts and feelings were becoming overwhelming. I suddenly shot straight up. I left the earth behind. I was floating in space, looking down on a blue and green earth. It looked so peaceful from up here.

I just wanted to clear my mind and not think. Every time I thought of something or someone, I was there. I needed to slow down.

I wanted to take a deep breath, but I realized I could not. I suddenly realized I had not been breathing for awhile. I did not need to breathe.

I looked down on the planet and thought how pretty it was. I looked around me and thought how pretty the stars and the moon looked.

I do not know how long I was there. It seemed like forever. Time stood still again. All was quiet.

****

Someone was with me. I could feel his presence. I suddenly realized that I had always felt his presence, all my life and that he was not human.

"*Who are you?*" I thought.

"*I am your guardian angel.*" Came the reply. It came as a thought gently placed into my head. There was no sound.

"*What is your name?*" I wondered.

"*You already know my name.*"

****

I was a little girl again, kneeling beside my bed to say my prayers with my mother. I climbed into bed, put my little arms around my mother's neck and kissed her good night. She stroked my hair gently.

"May your guardian angel watch over you tonight and protect you." My mother said, as always.

"What's my guardian angel's name?" I asked.

"Why don't you give him a name?" My mother asked.

"Can I do that?"

"Why not? My mother smiled.

"Alright." I knew I had to find the perfect name.

****

"*Pascal.*"

"*Yes.*" He replied. "*You chose very wisely.*"

"*I remember I liked it because it is an Easter name. I thought you would seem closer to God that way.*"

"*What is an angel?*" I wondered.

"*Spirit. Thought personified.*"

I thought I understood better now. It was one thing to be told angels were spirit and had no body, we still imagined them as shining men with wings.

I could not see Pascal, there was nothing to see. I could not hear him. I could not physically feel him. Had I wanted to, I would not be able to taste him or smell him.

"*Like thought,*" I said to myself, "*You cannot see, hear, feel, taste nor smell thought. Yet we know thought exists. We all think. Spirits are like pure thought, move by thought, communicate by thought…*"

"*God created the world by thought alone!*" I realized. "*Thought is very powerful. Well, His thought anyway.*"

"*Prayer is also very powerful.*" Pascal replied. "*More than you know. Many things have been won through constant prayer.*"

"*But so many things never change.*" I argued.

"*That is because you see with limited eyes. Sometimes the prayers of one generation are answered many generations later.* The people that walked in darkness have seen a great light. *It didn't happen right away. God promised a Messiah. In your eyes it took a very long time. But God is outside of time.*"

"*How can you tell people about God when they can't see Him, nor can they see an answer to prayer?*" I asked.

"*How do you know that God really does exist and that He is not just a silly story invented to either explain the inexplicable or in order to control other people?*" Pascal asked me.

"*Because I have a soul.*" I suddenly realized. "*Because I have developed it, prayed with it. We couldn't know God if we didn't have a soul. How could something purely physical ever know something purely spiritual?*"

"*Exactly.*" Pascal stated, "*You have a soul. You have fed that soul. You believe in God because your soul knows He exists. You cannot have a relationship with a Being and then doubt His existence.*"

"*The more I pray,*" I thought, "*The more time I spend in his presence, in communion with Him, the more I know God exists. I cannot prove it physically, but I know it spiritually.*"

"*If someone challenged me to prove God's existence, I should challenge him to pray.*" I mused. "*To know He exists, a person must pray. You will never know He exists if you choose to ignore that part of you. If you pray to God to show Himself,*" *and you remain open, He will. Your soul will know Him. You have to reach out to God with your soul. That is the only way to find Him, to know Him."*

At that moment, I could feel a great warmth. Not a physical warmth, but more like a very intense love penetrating me, surrounding me. It felt like warm light all around. I felt very drawn towards it.

"That's God I feel isn't it?" I thought.

"Yes."

"I want to go to Him."

"It isn't time yet." Pascal replied.

Suddenly I was back in the City. I could still feel Pascal's presence. It enveloped me. I realized his spirit surrounded mine, to better protect it. It had always been this way. I could still faintly feel the warmth of the presence of God, but now a chill went through me.

I saw a young boy, about eight or nine, looking at some toys a street vendor was selling. He held a tiny car in his fist. He looked around furtively.

Had I still been in my body, the hair on the back of my neck would have been standing straight up. I could feel a spiritual chill. Something evil was stalking. If I could have trembled, my teeth would have chattered loud enough to wake the dead. Nothing changed, but it seemed as though the light was now being filtered through something very black. It seemed to slither closer. Fear filled me.

"It cannot harm you." Pascal told me.

"What is it?!" I asked.

"Temptation." He replied. *"One of many who roam the earth looking for victims."*

"Demons?" I asked.

"Yes."

"But..."

"Human souls are made to resist temptation." Pascal told me. *"But they need guidance in their early years."*

"Cole!" A young woman walked towards the boy. Instantly the presence of evil departed. It had been thwarted.

"Put that back, Cole." The woman told the boy. "We are not getting anything today." Reluctantly, the boy placed the toy back on the shelf and turned to go with his mother.

"Some people can't get enough of the paranormal." I thought. *"If they only knew..."*

"There is a special relationship between the Church and Heaven." Pascal told me, *"There is so much that is* paranormal *as you say. For example, stigmatics like Saint Padre Pio."*

****

In an instant, we were in a large beautifully decorated church. Light filtered through stained-glass windows, depicting scenes from the gospels and various saints. Behind the altar, a huge crucifix, with a suffering Jesus hung in the center. The Tabernacle was below it, on the altar, which was placed against the wall.

The place was full of people wearing clothes that were strange to me. I thought maybe we were in the 20th or 21st century.

"1960." Pascal affirmed.

At the front of the church, priests were celebrating mass. I moved closer and noticed the main celebrant. He was an older man, with graying hair and a mostly white beard that came down to the top of his chest. The more I looked at him the more he stood out. He was so concentrated on the consecration of the mass that he seemed almost in a trance.

Then I noticed his hands. They were covered with some kind of wrapping and I could see blood stains on them.

"He's bleeding!"

"Yes."

"This is Padre Pio!"

"Yes." I could sense the humour in Pascal. He thought I was a little slow.

I watched the priest in awe. I could sense the goodness emanating from him like a flood. But then I could sense also the presence of many invisible evil beings. They were jealousy, hatred, pride, egoism and countless others.

I could sense them on the outside, they could not get close. They hated Padre Pio and the people who were there.

I suddenly got an idea of the kind of spiritual battles this man must have, for the holier a person was, the more these demons seemed to want to attack. I understood, as one sometimes understands things suddenly in a dream, with out being told, that this holy priest had been attacked with accusations of insanity, immoral behaviour, misuse of funds, that he had also been attacked both spiritually and physically by demons, and that he suffered greatly from illnesses as well as from the stigmata.

For a brief moment, I found myself in a small room that had little more than a chair, a desk and a bed in it. At the desk, seated on the chair, a slightly younger Padre Pio was writing a letter to someone. I read part of it.

I saw before me a mysterious person similar to the one I had seen on the evening of 5 August. The only difference was that his hands and feet and side were dripping blood. This sight terrified me and what I felt at that moment is indescribable. I thought I should have died if the Lord had not intervened and strengthened my heart which was about to burst out of my chest. The vision disappeared and I became aware that my hands, feet and side were dripping blood. Imagine the agony I experienced and continue to experience almost every day. The heart wound bleeds continually, especially from Thursday evening until Saturday. Dear Father, I am dying of pain because of the wounds and the resulting embarrassment I feel deep in my soul. I am afraid I shall bleed to death if the Lord does not hear my heartfelt supplication to relieve me of this condition. Will Jesus, who is so good, grant me this grace? Will he at least free me from the embarrassment caused by these outward signs? I will raise my voice and will not stop imploring him until in his mercy he takes away, not the wound or the pain, which is impossible since I wish to be inebriated with pain, but these outward signs which cause me such embarrassment and unbearable humiliation.

"There are also saints that have been known to levitate." Pascal said. *"Like Saint Joseph of Cupertino."*

****

Late afternoon light cast long shadows from the vines that grew in a large field. A small procession wound its way down a dirt road, passing through the vineyards on either side. It was late in the season and most of the grapes had now been picked.

By the way people were dressed, the women in drably coloured long skirts, with shawls and head coverings, and the men in simple wooden shoes, leggings and tunics, I knew we must be sometime in the medieval ages.

"*1630.*" Came the answer from Pascal.

The people were chanting in a language I guessed was Italian, and as I looked closer, I saw that the statue being carried in front was one of St Francis of Assisi.

"*It is the feast day of Saint Francis.*" Pascal told me.

There were a few friars leading the procession, one of which was holding the statue. The oldest friar immediately behind him was holding a book of prayers.

I looked again, more closely this time, one of the younger friars seemed to be gliding along, rather than walking, as if he were being pulled on wheels. A quick look at his feet showed me that there were no wheels under his feet, and his feet were quite simply not touching the ground!

The young friar soared into the air, amid gasps from people around him. He did not appear to be aware of what was happening, but only stared into space, lost in his thoughts or perhaps seeing something that no one else could?

Noting the excitement around him, the friar suddenly came back to himself, realized what was happening, and thus descended immediately. He appeared to be very ill at ease, and bothered by the attention being given to him by the others, for he quickly ran off and disappeared, leaving everyone behind him in an uproar.

"*How about statues that leak tears and blood?*" Pascal asked once again.

****

Images of numerous statues and paintings, all crying tears or blood, or bleeding from the hands, feet, side and head flashed through my thoughts.

"*Visionaries?*"

****

I saw Bernadette in Lourdes, Jacinta, Francisco and Lucia in Fatima, and flashes of many others I did not know, all in what seemed to be a trance, unaware of anything that was going on around them, intent only on what it was they were seeing.

"*Incorruptibles?*" Pascal continued.

****

We were in a small graveyard, in a northern country. The graveyard was surrounded by evergreens. Wildflowers dotted the landscape. What seemed to be some kind of school or residence was nearby. It was a simple wooden building, not the impressive structures of Europe.

Some people were digging out a few of the graves, and talking about relocating them to a different graveyard. They were dark-skinned mostly, and had very different features from what I was used to. Native North Americans, I decided.

"Carrier people of Northern British Columbia." Pascal affirmed. "The year is 1951."

A yell went up from one of the men moving a coffin. The lid had moved and the native woman inside was still in perfect condition!

"Rose Prince!" One of them exclaimed. "She's been dead for two years!"

The other coffins were examined and all the other bodies were in various degrees of decomposition, even those buried after Rose Prince.

"*What about miracles connected with communion hosts?*" Pascal asked again. "*The proof is there, if you are willing to see it.*"

"*Yes*" I replied, "*But if you refuse to believe, you can dismiss it all. Visionaries are crazy people who hear voices and hallucinate. Stigmatics are people who self-*

mutilate, the religious statues are in humid places, or some other logical scientific reason is causing something looking like blood to pour out of them non-stop. The perfectly preserved bodies of saints are pure coincidence, some freak accident of nature that caused them to be preserved. Where is the proof that anyone levitated? People will believe anything. Catholics are a bunch of lunatics."

"You know," I thought, *"When I was young, I used to wonder why God only talked to people in the Old Testament. I wondered what was wrong with the world today that He no longer appeared to people. It is just that you have to know where to look and you will see that there are still prophets today, to whom God speaks or sends messengers from Heaven."*

"Yes." Pascal replied, *"In fact, there are an amazing number of people today who receive messages in one form or another from Heaven. Miracles happen everyday. People have forgotten that a miracle happens at every mass on that altar. Mass easily becomes something commonplace. People do not realize WHO it is they are eating. If they did, they would lay prostrate on the floor at the consecration."*

"I know," I sighed. *"I have done it too. I cannot imagine Sunday without mass. It is my addiction, my spiritual food. Sunday would not be Sunday if I did not attend mass. But I forget who it is that is on the altar."*

I wondered what it would be like to live without that miracle, to never receive Christ physically into one's body, or worse yet, to never receive him spiritually, never truly believe in him, never understand his message, never feel that higher calling, never believe in a higher purpose, never want only good for others.

I wondered what it would be like to be Garrick.

****

A young boy stood at a kitchen counter. His mother laughed at his efforts to drag a heavy chair to stand on. She leaned over to grab the back of the chair.

"Let me help you Garrick!"

The boy grinned at his mother and she patted his cheek.

"Here," she said, "Stir this in."

Little Garrick stood on his chair stirring ingredients as his mother poured them into a huge aluminum bowl. Lively music played, and the mother smiled tenderly at her son.

****

A slightly older Garrick sat on a wooden chair, staring at the inert woman on the hospital bed. By the way the light fell through the window, I could tell it was late afternoon. There was no breeze, the yellow and green curtains were still. It was hot. The forehead of his mother, now much thinner, much paler, and suddenly much older, was moist, and the collar of Garrick's shirt was wet with sweat.

Garrick's face was streaked with tears. His father, much younger than when I had known him, stalked into the room.

"Tears won't help you boy," he said shortly, "Dry those up now, and be a man."

****

Garrick and his father stood in front of a closed casket in the Cathedral of the City. Garrick kept sneaking peeks up at his father, who was talking to another man. I could see he was trying not to cry.

"…she was a religious woman, my wife." Garrick's father was saying, "so I'll let her have this last visit to a church; her funeral. But her faith didn't do her any good. She's dead now. We won't be coming back." He looked down at Garrick. "Stop your sniveling boy!"

****

The sun shone bright in the school yard. Garrick stood beside his two friends Paul and Amir. His face was hard now, cynical. He sneered at the smaller, skinnier boy in front of him.

"You're worth nothing, Asur. You can't even throw a ball straight. Look at you, you're no better than a dung beetle. You'll never be a man, you've got no muscles!"

179

Asur turned away. The boys laughed. A group of young people had now gathered to watch.

Garrick grabbed Asur by the shoulder and turned him around.

"You're ugly, you know that? You're not a dung beetle, you're the piece of shit it eats!"

More boys started to snicker now.

Garrick raised his voice. "Who here thinks Asur, the piece of shit will ever get himself a girl? What girl in her right mind would want to kiss something that ugly?"

I saw myself push through the crowd that had formed. I was livid. I marched up to Garrick and stared him in the face. He looked down at me condescendingly.

"You are the ugly one Garrick Sanche!" I proclaimed. "The more crap you speak, the more like crap you look! So who's the ugly dung-beetle now? What girl in her right mind would want to kiss someone who speaks shit and looks like it? You make me sick. No girl could kiss you and not be sick after!"

I turned around and looked at Asur

"*I* like you Asur." I said, "You are kind and gentle, and you are *not* ugly!" I pulled his face down to mine to prove it and kissed him right on the mouth.

Asur looked stunned. Then he smiled, ever so softly at Garrick and turned to walk away.

Garrick wanted to hit us, I knew, but a teacher had come over to see what was going on. I watched as his face turned red with rage.

I saw him walk home and enter the house. His father sat reading a newspaper in the living room.

"Why can't you be like other boys?" His father's voice boomed out. "You'll never amount to anything boy. You don't get good grades, you learn nothing, and you can't even get a girl to kiss you, but a loser like that Midfallah boy can!"

He looked up at Garrick now, so as not to lose out on seeing the astonishment in his son's face.

"Yes, I know all about what goes on in that schoolyard boy." Garrick's father sneered. "I had plenty of girls before your mother, and you can't even get one."

****

"It's time to go." I could almost feel Pascal nudge me. *"You are being called."*

I suddenly realized I had been hearing voices, one voice in particular, for quite some time now.

The voice was familiar. I focused on it.

"Isabella," it pleaded, "Come back! Please!" It was like a magnet. Somehow his soul had latched on to mine and was dragging me back.

"Asur!" I no longer resisted. In an instant I was there, floating just above my body. It was now hooked up to beeping machines inside of what appeared to be some kind of vehicle. Asur held my hand in his, and looked desperate.

II

The pain suddenly came back. For a moment, it was unbearable. I moaned.

"She's back." I heard a voice say.

"Isabella!" Asur's voice trembled. I opened my eyes. His face seemed to float in front of mine.

I wanted to say something, but I seemed to be having a very hard time breathing. The pain left. My body seemed to have numbed itself to pain. I felt drugged.

"Don't try to talk." The other voice said. "You may have a pierced lung. Just rest. Help is on its way."

Ambulances are one of the few motorized vehicles left. In some cities like San Isidor, there are a few electrical tramways that take you from one neighbourhood to another, for those that need to get somewhere more quickly than on foot or with a carriage. I've never needed to take one yet. Peacekeepers also have a few motorcars that run on electricity, for emergencies.

It was getting harder to keep my eyes open. The feeling of being drugged was getting stronger and it was making me want to sleep.

"Stay with me Isabella." Asur told me, "Don't leave again."

I blinked my eyes. "Tired." My lips formed the word, but very little sound came out. Asur leaned closer.

"Tired." I tried again.

"She says she's tired." Asur said in answer to the paramedic's question.

"Let her sleep." He replied.

"Close your eyes then, Princess." Asur murmured. "I'll stand guard."

I managed a faint smile before I closed my eyes and drifted off to sleep.

****

I woke briefly in a hospital room. Asur was still with me. There were IV's running into my arms. It was still difficult to breathe, and I still had an oxygen mask over my face. My back throbbed.

Asur looked tired and worried. He smiled at me when he saw that I was awake. He took my hand and squeezed it, but did not say anything. I smiled back at him, trying to reassure him.

Only a few minutes passed and I was tired of being awake. I longed to get away from the pain and the breathlessness I felt. I closed my eyes again.

****

I do not know how much time passed. I only know that time passed. I was not aware of much.

When I became aware of myself again, all was dark. I seemed to be floating in darkness. I could not move. I seemed to hear voices from some outside world, but I was trapped in the darkness. It was as if I was trapped within my own head.

"It's been a week and she is still not responding." I heard a faint voice say, from that outside world. "You should think about what you want to do if she never comes back."

"I want to give her time." Said an equally faint but familiar voice. Another voice, a woman's this time, that also seemed familiar asked, "Do you think she might never come back?"

"*Do you want to go back?*" Came a thought in my head. "*I can get you there.*"

"*Back?*" I thought "*Is it me they're talking of? Can I get out there?*"

"*Of course silly girl.*" Came the answer.

There was something wrong with this being. Something I did not quite like nor trust, but I could not figure out why exactly.

"*Your soul is trapped here, but I can bring it back out there.*"

"*How? What do I have to do?*"

"*I need you to agree to do certain things for me on the other side.*"

"*What things?*"

"Nothing complicated. Just some small things."

"Like what?"

"I have some souls to help."

The blackness receded just enough for me to glimpse the image of a man. He had an ageless quality. He was not young, his eyes were too deep, too full of experience and knowledge for him to be young, yet his face had no wrinkle and his hair had no grey in it.

He smiled at me, wanting to seem reassuring.

"Let us conclude an agreement," he said.

"I will get you out of here, so you can help some people get out of hardship they cannot endure anymore."

"What kind of hardship?" I wanted to know.

"Poverty for the most part." He replied. "Physical suffering. The details are not important just yet."

He had a piece of paper in his left hand. His right hand produced a pen.

"I want you to sign here, to accept our little contract," he said.

I took the pen and the paper. The contract seemed to be written in some foreign or ancient language.

As I put the pen to the paper, it suddenly seemed as if a thousand voices, were screaming in my mind *"No!"*

I realized in that moment that this must be the devil or a demon in front of me and I called out the first name that came to my mind. *"God!"*

Instantly, something like a strong wind rushed in. The demon was thrown backwards with a great force and disappeared, as did both the paper and pen in my hand.

I could feel the familiar enveloping presence around me again.

"You are with me?"

"I am always with you." Came Pascal's reply. *"Just as God is always with you. You only need call His name."*

"Why could I not feel your presence?" I asked.

"You were too focused on something else. You will not always feel my presence. You will not always feel God's presence. But we will always be with you."

"Who were the people screaming in my head?" I asked.

"The communion of saints."

****

More days passed. Sometimes I slept. But always, when I woke, I was in that black world. Sometimes I could hear voices from the outer world. There were three voices I heard more often than others.

"How long will it take?" moaned the woman's voice.

"Be patient Mrs. Campanare." Came the younger man's voice. "Have faith. Her body needs to heal, perhaps this is the way it has to be, for her to heal."

"The doctor thinks we should let her go." The older man said.

"I know I do not have the right to decide, since our wedding was annulled," said the younger man, "but I beg you please, to give her more time. I am certain she is stronger than this."

"The doctor thinks it is useless to keep her alive much longer." Said the older man.

I wondered who they were talking about. I hoped they would give whoever it was, the time she needed.

"She is healing, is she not?" the younger man said. "Her lung is all closed, almost healed. She isn't suffering from a pneumothorax anymore. She won't need extra oxygen much longer. Her heartbeat is much better. She just needs a bit of time." -

I slept again, and when I awoke, the younger man was talking.

"Isabella, I beg you, you have to come back." He pleaded. "You are a strong woman. Your life is not over. It is just beginning. You have already given so much, but you have much more to give. I don't know if you can hear me..." Here his voice broke a bit and trailed off. "But if you can, you need to find your way back here, somehow, and you need to do it fast. You need to show us that there is still someone left to save. Before it is too late."

I felt sorry for the young man. He seemed so sad. I wanted to comfort him somehow. I wanted to make him feel better. I hoped the person he was talking to would find her way back to him.

"Isabella, I am holding your hand." came his voice again. "If you are in there, if you can hear me, if you can feel me, please let me know, somehow."

I wanted to take his hand. I wanted to squeeze it. But I was still in this black world, I did not know how to get to that other world.

I concentrated very hard on my hands. For awhile, I felt nothing, then suddenly I felt warmth surrounding my right hand. Someone was holding on to my right hand! The more I focused on that hand, the more I could physically feel the other hand surrounding it. In that instant I knew that he was talking to me and that I was the girl named Isabella. With all the force I had, I concentrated on squeezing the hand that held mine.

It was like being yanked through an abyss, like spinning through a tunnel towards light. I felt like I was being pulled back into the world.

The pressure on my hand increased. I could feel his breath on my cheek as he whispered in my ear. "Isabella, come back."

I opened my eyes and this time, instead of the dark I saw a green hospital room with curtains pulled back from the window through which light from the late afternoon sun was spilling in. I could hear beeping of equipment and noises from the hallway, people talking.

I turned my head to the right and looked into Asur's golden brown eyes.

"Oh thank God!" Was all he said, before he laid his forehead on my chest.

I brought my hands, hands that moved when I willed them to move, up to his head and ran my fingers through his hair. He turned his head to face me and I stroked his cheek.

He looked much thinner than when I had last seen him. He also looked very tired.

"You don't look so good." I said.

He threw his head back and laughed. "If you think I don't look so good," he said. "You don't want to look in a mirror."

I smiled. "How long have I been here?" I asked.

"Two weeks."

"She's back!" my mother's voice exclaimed from the doorway.

She rushed over to smother me with kisses. My father stood behind her, looking very pleased.

There was a sudden flurry of activity, as a nurse came in, realized what had happened, and called for the doctor and more staff.

There was a lot talking, most of which I did not understand, involving medical terms and medication and dosages of this and that, and in the middle of it all, my stomach started to growl.

"I just want to know," I said as soon as there was a lull in the conversation, "when I get to eat."

There was some laughter at that. They seemed to be rather pleased that I wanted to eat.

"We can arrange for that right away." The doctor said.

What did end up on my supper tray was not the appetizing supper I had imagined.

"Purée." The nurse said apologetically. I'm afraid your stomach can't handle more than that."

In the end, Asur ended up spoon feeding it to me, because my hands shook too much. I decided that I was going make sure that he did not have to do that for very long.

III

It only took a day or so before I was able to feed myself without spilling.

Breathing was painful, and the wound in my back still hurt, but I was glad to be alive and thus I was able to endure it gladly.

Asur told me that I had been stabbed in the back, and had hit my head on a rock when I had fallen. I had also been trampled on, in the melee that had ensued when the peacekeepers had run in to apprehend Garrick and his men.

The knife had pierced my right lung and caused a pneumothroax. Air had built up around the lungs and caused the right one to collapse. I had stopped breathing. Luckily for me, paramedics had arrived within minutes and a needle had been placed into my chest to decompress the pneumothorax. My heart had been restarted with a defibrillator and I had started breathing on my own again, shortly after. I had been put on oxygen and taken to the hospital.

Alberto, Maria and Erin came in later that day to visit. Alberto was healing well. He had a few bruised ribs and some deep cuts. "I'm sorry this happened to you." I told him, when I was able to.

"It is not a problem." Alberto replied, "I am just happy that no one is dead."

Maria came back the next day to visit alone. She offered to stay with me while Asur left to shower and eat or rest if he wanted to. He seemed to sense that she wanted to be alone with me, and after saying goodbye, he stepped quietly out of the room.

Maria sat in the armchair beside my bed. She folded her hands in front of her and looked at them for a moment. Then she raised her head and looked up at me.

"Alberto is not the same since what happened," she said.

"Is that good or bad?" I asked.

"So far it is good." She replied. "He seems to be more open in some way. I don't quite understand what is different, but something is."

"He wants us to spend this evening together alone. He says Gabriela is old enough to watch the other two now. He hasn't proposed anything like that since before we were married!"

"Well that's good!" I exclaimed.

"Yes I know," sighed Maria, "But do you know what the strange thing is? I am so used to being always disappointed that we never do anything together and that he doesn't seem to care much about me that now I would rather not do anything. I can't bring myself to be happy or excited that we are going out together."

She stared out the window for awhile. I said nothing.

"I do not know if it is just pride or spitefulness on my part or fear that I am just going to be disappointed again. I think a lot of it is just me being spiteful."

She looked at me. "I think it is me wanting to get back at him by telling him: you wanted things to be this way, so now if you don't like how things turned out, too bad for you!"

Maria leaned back in her chair. "What do you think?" she asked.

"I think he may have experienced something back there, he came close to dying, we both did. Maybe things have changed for him now."

"Maybe." Maria muttered. "But I don't want to give him an easy time. He's not just going to suddenly start giving me flowers and have everything perfect."

"Has he been giving you flowers?" I asked.

"He did, once." She sighed again. "I had to force myself to smile and thank him. I suppose he noticed I wasn't very enthusiastic, but at least I didn't impatiently ask him why he'd done it, which is what I *wanted* to do."

"The thing is," She continued, "for me, flowers from him are meaningless. Flowers from anyone else show me that the person wanted to please me in some way. Flowers from him indicate he felt somehow obliged to do *some*thing for me, just because it's a required thing, because it's expected, because he should be doing something, not because he *wants* to. He's never really wanted to before, except maybe the first few months we knew each other. After that, he made it plain that gift-giving and doing things for each other were superficial and unnecessary, and that I should not expect anything from him, nor he from me."

"I have this thing." Maria said, "This letter I wrote him, saying how I felt and how I would like things to be. I have held on to it now for almost four years. I never gave it to him. I could never bring myself to give it to him. Why should I share an intimate part of myself with him when he rejects intimacy?"

"You're afraid to give it to him?"

"Not afraid." Maria insisted. "At least, not afraid of being hurt. He would not hurt me. That much I know."

She got up to pace the room. "Maybe I am afraid of something. I don't know what. I don't want to give someone an intimate part of me and have it just, I don't know, go to waste? I'm jealous of who I am. I don't like to just go around sharing who I am with people. I don't want to give something away to someone who won't receive it and care about it."

"Well, you don't have to make any decisions right away." I said. "Go out with your husband. Make up your mind to have fun, in spite of him. I'll pray for you."

An idea occurred to me suddenly, "Ask your guardian angel to guide you, to pray for you." I told her.

"My guardian angel?"

"Who else knows you better, besides God?" I asked her. "Who else is better placed to know what to pray for, for you?"

****

I was released from the hospital in just a few days, with orders to take it easy. The lung was almost healed, most of the healing had taken place while I was in a coma. It was enough to make breathing difficult, but not impossible. It was not the reason I had been in a coma, that was due, the doctor said, mostly to the way I had fallen. I had apparently hit the side of my head on something hard. I had also sustained some minor injuries due to people tripping over me and stepping on me in the struggle with the peacekeepers.

The only problem now, was where to go. "I've been to your apartment Bella, and I started packing some of your things, so you can come back home with us when we leave tomorrow." My mother told me.

This irritated me a little, as she had not asked me first, and had assumed I was going back to the City, when in fact, I was not certain that I wanted to go back.

"Mother," I said gently, "I appreciate that, but I am not certain that I want to go home to the City with you."

"But Bella, Meloncillo…" my mother's voice trailed off as she looked at my father. The last time I remember my mother calling me Meloncillo, I had still been a child, wearing a brightly coloured scarf in my hair to shade my head from the sun, and toting a heavy satchel full of books to school. It is a pet name for children that is fairly common in the City. The real meloncillo is a type of mongoose that thrives in the arid climate around the City.

My father looked at me. "Bella, you know you are being released from the hospital, but not from care. Your apartment is too small for all of us to stay in including Leticia. You need people to take care of you. We are only thinking in practical terms."

He was right. I did not like it, but he was right. "You can come back in the fall to continue your studies if you like." My mother said.

"Do you want to continue?" My father asked, "After all, once you are married," he looked pointedly at me, "*again*, to Asur, you will not need to work."

"Father," I said patiently, "not *again*, but *for real* this time."

I hesitated a moment and then said, "I may not need to work once I am married, but I still wish to be an educated woman. I may appreciate it some day. I may be able to use it some day. And I believe," I looked at Asur, "That my fiancé enjoys having intellectual discussions with a woman who is informed on different topics."

"Absolutely." Asur, who had been quiet until now, affirmed.

"At the end of this current semester, I would have only had one year left of studies." I continued. I would like to try to take some summer classes to catch up a bit and try to finish before Christmas of next year if possible."

I took Asur's hand in mine. "We'll have to talk." I said simply. He nodded. For the first time, I noticed the way his thick dark lashes almost brushed his cheeks when he blinked. I had always thought him quite good-looking, but in that moment, he was stunningly handsome to me. His cheeks had hollowed out and his jaw seemed to me to be more defined than ever. I could see slight creases in his forehead, from frowning when he was worried about something. He was not a large man, but he had good shoulders. His hair had grown a little on the long side and it waved slightly at the collar. I was struck by a sudden urge to be alone with him and run my fingers through his thick, dark brown locks.

Instead, I tore my eyes away from him and turned back to my parents.

"I will come home with you." I said. "For now. We will decide later what I will do. But I don't want to leave tomorrow. I have friends I want to say goodbye to."

A room was rented adjacent to the ones Asur and my parents had been renting on the first floor of a nearby Inn. I was brought over in a wheelchair, and made comfortable in one of the small salons. Plants livened up the room and a couple of beautiful painting graced the blue walls. Other people sat in corners of the room talking quietly. Some food was brought in and set down on the table beside me.

Asur sat down on one of the armchairs beside me. He leaned back into the chair, closed his eyes and sighed. "I have to say," he said, with his eyes still closed, "These chairs are much more comfortable than the hospital ones."

I smiled tenderly at him. I was just so glad to have him there.

"I have a lot to tell you." I said.

Asur opened his eyes. "Tell me," he said.

I told him about Pascal, and seeing all the different saints across the ages and what it was like being all spirit with no body to keep you on the ground. Then I told him about Garrick.

"You think all of this is real?" Asur asked, "And not some kind of..."

"Hallucination?" I finished for him, when he hesitated.

"Well, yes." He admitted.

"Asur," I said looking straight into his eyes, "I am almost certain that what I experienced was real and not some kind of hallucination, but there is only one way to find out."

"You'll have to verify facts," he said.

"Yes."

I stared out the window, from where I was sitting, I could see a fairly busy side-street, lined with trees. Neighbours greeted each other, children played in a front yard, and people walked past.

"I want to visit Garrick." I said.

"Garrick?! In prison?"

"Yes." I said, turning to look back at Asur. "I want to apologize for what I said that day."

Asur looked stunned. Then he threw back his head and laughed.

"You have succeeded in amazing me once more," he said.

"So, you'll come with me?" I asked.

"Wouldn't miss it." He replied.

****

Asur, my parents and I met Alberto, Maria, Erin and the children at a quiet restaurant on Avenida San Martin.

The hostess at the door led us through a dining room that was only half-filled with people quietly chatting over lunch. Paintings from various artists hung on the half-brick, half-plaster walls. Low ceiling lights hung over each table and towards the back, lamps hung on the wall in a corridor which the hostess led us through towards two open French doors.

The back terrace was almost empty of people, only a few couples sat here and there. It was a lush garden, with a pergola immediately overhead and another in the far corner. A large tree stood in the middle of it, with wooden benches built in a pentagon around it. Plants hung everywhere from the pergolas, and tables and comfortable garden chairs were tastefully arranged around huge pots of all kinds of flowering plants and trees.

The hostess led us to a secluded area, under the far pergola. With all the plants around us, noise did not travel very far and it seemed as if we were alone in the place. I looked around and let my eyes soak in the beauty, the white iron-wrought garden tables and chairs, the deep red, cream and gold of the paisley-patterned cushions, the different, vibrantly coloured flowers. The air was sweet and heavy with nectar and I could hear the busy buzzing of bees.

Asur pulled out one of the garden chairs and invited me to sit in it. I sank down into the luxurious softness of its cushions and sighed contentedly. I noticed Alberto doing the same for Maria, who looked mildly surprised and then nearly burst out laughing at the expression of disbelief on Gabriela's face. Apparently, it was out of character for Alberto to do such a thing.

It was not, however, out of character for my father to do so, and I almost laughed again at the sight of my mother waiting in front of her chair for my father to come around and seat her. It amused me to see such differences in culture and personality.

The waiter arrived, dressed in elegant black and white, with the menus, explained the specials of the day and invited us to order something to drink to start.

My mother asked my father if he would prefer white wine or an aperitif. He thought he would take advantage of the occasion to have something special and go with an aperitif. So my mother ordered a Pineau des Charentes for him and a sangria for herself. The waiter looked slightly startled but said nothing and noted the requests.

Alberto leaned across Maria, who sat next to me and asked me, "Does your father not have a mind of his own? Why does your mother order for him?"

I smiled. "Tradition." I said. "In the City, it is traditional for the women of the upper classes to serve their men. It is the mark of a married woman, especially in public. A wife takes pride in serving her husband, in knowing his tastes and serving him what he enjoys most. It is one of the ways in which we show our affection by demonstrating how well we pay attention to their taste. If we were in the City, you would sit across from Maria, not beside her, and this way all would know that you were a couple. This is how it is done in high society, however the middle classes do not follow such rules."

"I see." Alberto replied. "Here, it is the opposite, a man orders the drinks for himself and for the woman he accompanies."

I chuckled. "It is no wonder then, that our waiter seemed slightly shocked.

Maria smiled and looked at the waiter, who was now taking orders for drinks from the children.

Alberto ordered white wine for himself and for Maria, and Asur asked me, "Shall I or shall you?"

"When in Rome, do as the Romans." I replied.

"What may I order for you then, my lady?" he asked with a flourish.

"White wine." I replied.

Our drinks arrived shortly, our orders were taken and we were left alone to chat while the food was prepared.

Alberto, Asur and my father were in the middle of a big discussion about international business, when Maria leaned closer to me and said softly, "I told you Alberto was going to take me out for dinner the other night…"

"Yes?"

"We went to this small place, not many people around. He wanted to talk."

"And?"

"And he told me that he was not sure why, but he had noticed that things had gradually changed between us over the years. He didn't notice it at first, then thought it was normal, with the arrival of children and the settling into domestic life. But then he realized there was a deepening distance between us. Something was pulling us apart and he did not know what it was. He started to work harder to become a better provider, so he could fix the problem, but that did not fix it. The distance was still there, and it seemed to grow greater instead."

She paused. Her fingers traced the pattern on the tablecloth. I waited.

She turned to look at me again. "When he woke up in the hospital and saw me sitting there, it hit him. He thought I looked very sad. Not a temporary sadness to see him lying there, but a deep, profound sadness.

The kind of sadness that stays in a person's eyes even as they are laughing and chatting with friends. Then he said he suddenly realized that I had been sad for a very long time, but that he had not always known me that way. I used to laugh with my eyes when he first knew me, and now I no longer did."

Maria glanced over at Alberto to check that he was still absorbed in his conversation with Asur and my father, then looked back at me.

"He said he did not know what he had done to make me sad, but that he was certain that it had to be him. It couldn't logically be anyone else. He didn't think that it was the children. I seemed to be closer to them than to him. Or perhaps, he thought, it was not something he had done, but something he had not done?"

"What did you tell him?" I asked.

"I couldn't tell him anything." She admitted. "I am so used to keeping it all to myself that I could not tell him anything. I finally told him that I needed some time to think it over. I told him I was glad he had taken me out to dinner, and that I appreciated some time alone with him. I think I will have to take the thing I wrote for him out of hiding and give it to him."

"Do it." I squeezed her hand. "From what I know of Alberto, I think he is ready for it, and you will not regret it."

"I hope you are right." She answered.

I glanced over at Alberto, and in that moment I saw him turn and for a short moment look at Maria with such a look of tenderness and yearning that it made tears come to my eyes.

"I am sure that I am right." I replied.

The food arrived at that moment and our attention was turned on it and our empty stomachs.

Asur's hand lay on the table, across from me. He had done as was tradition in the City, and had sat across from me. I had finished eating and he was eating the last of his seafood paella, a delicious rice dish, typical in San Isidor because of its proximity to the ocean and therefore its access to all kinds of seafood.

Asur was now politely discussing musical tastes with Gabriela, who sat beside him, across from Maria. I slid my own hand across the table and entwined my fingers around his. He paused in mid-sentence to smile at me and turned back to Gabriela to discuss the merits of one of her favourite young musical artists who happened to be from the City.

I was sad to be leaving these wonderful people who I had grown to love as family. This very afternoon, I would once again be taking the shuttle, this time back to the City, which seemed to me, a lifetime away, a foreign concept. I had spent two whole years in this beautiful, fertile, luscious land and I was going back to a place that seemed to me to be a dream. Part of me wanted to stay. Part of me was glad that I no longer had to hide from danger and could live near my parents freely once again.

The Morales family with Erin accompanied us to the shuttle after we left the restaurant. Erin hugged me tight and joked about coming after us if we didn't come back.

Maria hugged me quietly, and smiled to hide her tears. Gabriela and the children said their goodbyes, and Alberto and I exchanged the customary two kisses, one on each cheek. Asur and Alberto shook hands, and then Maria hugged Asur goodbye.

I remembered the day I arrived in this place, and how foreign and exotic it had all seemed. It was hard to believe that I was going home again. San Isidor had been home for so long. And yet in just a few short minutes, I would be in a totally different world.

IV

A clock chimed two o'clock somewhere. A slight breeze drifted in through the window and lifted loose tendrils of hair at the back of my neck. It was very hot as usual in the City, but it was not unbearable like the humidity in San Isidor. I barely noticed the heat, although I was grateful for the breeze.

I sat on a very uncomfortable chair in the prison warden's office. Asur sat beside me in what seemed to be an equally uncomfortable chair, as he shifted position for the umpteenth time.

The only thing decorating the walls here was a calendar from one of the markets in the Bowl. The warden was in another room, consulting with his superior over the com system about whether or not I should be let in to see Garrick. The warden did not like the idea at all, but at our persistence, he agreed to consult his superior.

"Are you still sure you want to do this? Asur asked me.

I nodded, even though I was starting to have misgivings.

The warden, a middle-aged, thin, balding man with a very trim mustache entered the room. He held himself erect as he walked across the room and sat down across from with perfect posture.

He crossed his hands in front of him, and then uncrossed them.

"My superior has granted your request." He told us.

Relief and then fear gripped me. Asur took my hand.

The warden stood up. "If you would follow me." He invited us.

"In a minute please." I said. "Could you give me just a minute to prepare myself?"

"As you wish." He replied. "I will be waiting outside." He walked to the door and stepped out.

Asur looked at me. "You don't have to do this," he said. "You can back out if you want."

"No," I said. "I have to."

Where, I thought, *are you Pascal. I need you here, now. I need you to help me, to keep me safe. How will I know what to say? Please, somehow, pray to God to give me some kind of peace.*

In that instant, I felt a reassuring presence. I felt as I had felt as a child, when my father would lift me up at the end of the day and rock me as he read a story to me. I felt the way I felt when my mother wrapped her arms around me and held me tight. Someone, some presence was wrapped all around me, holding me tight.

Give me peace. I thought. *Tell me what I have to say.*

A prickling feeling crawled up my neck. My mind cleared. I was no longer afraid. I stood up.

"I am ready." I said.

Asur stood up.

"This is something I should do alone." I replied. "Will you stay here and pray?"

Asur frowned.

"Please?" I asked. "It just feels more...right, this way."

"All right." He replied.

The warden led me down quiet, bare hallways, to a first set of locked doors. Guards sat in chairs, playing a card game on the other side.

We went through a second set of locked doors and now we walked through corridors lined with prison cells and doors with barred windows. Most inmates sat quietly in their cells, but a few stood and stared. Some made lewd comments and one or two insulted me.

"Ignore them." The warden said.

We walked through a third set of locked doors. Security was higher here. There were more guards and one of them came to accompany us.

I was brought to a room divided into two by a pane of plexi-glass. There was a hole in the middle, covered in some kind of fine mesh, so one could to talk to people on the other side. A chair sat on my side of the room. The warden invited me to sit. He and the guard left the room and closed the door, which was almost entirely made of glass. They would not hear our conversation, but they could see through the glass, and would watch in case I needed them.

I sat there waiting, still feeling euphoric and at peace, and trying to concentrate only on the presence I felt all around me and not on my fear of seeing Garrick again.

The door on the other side of the room, on the other side of the glass panel, opened and a guard escorted Garrick to the chair across from me.

Garrick looked quite startled to see me, but recovered quickly and sneered at me as the guard handcuffed him to his chair. The guard then left the room and we were alone to talk.

Garrick spoke first.

"Have you come to request an apology then?" he asked sarcastically.

I stared at him for a moment, took in the hard lines around his mouth, the anger in his eyes.

"No," I replied slowly, clearly. "I have come to apologize to you."

This time the startled look stayed on his face a bit longer.

He scowled then, "What...what kind of joke is this?" He demanded. "I don't want to talk to you! Guard!" he turned his head to the door.

"Wait!" I commanded. He turned around to look back at me. I leaned closer to the window and looked straight into his eyes.

"I am totally serious." I said. "When I was a child, I said something to you that I regret now. I was angry. I did not think my words could hurt you, I only wished to defend someone I liked."

"I told you, you looked like crap." I said. "I told you the more you spoke the more you looked like crap. I told you no girl could kiss you and not be sick afterwards."

Garrick glared back at me.

"I am sorry." I said. "I had no idea what your father was like. I had no idea why you tormented us. I did not know you were unhappy. I should never have said such a thing. Not even in defense of my friend. It is not true that you were crap, Garrick. I was mad you were picking on my friend. But other girls might have liked you. Other girls might have kissed you and enjoyed it."

"What do you know about my father and what he was like?" Garrick growled.

"I saw him." I said. "When I almost died last month."

Something like a flicker of guilt flashed in his eyes.

"I went back in time, back in space." I said. "I was all over." Our eyes were locked.

"I saw your father sitting in your living room when you came home that day after school." I said. "He laughed at you. He insulted you, he said he'd had many women before your mother and yet you couldn't even get a girl to kiss you when that Midfallah boy could."

"How could you know that?" Garrick's voice was very cold. "No one was there. No one knew. How could you know?"

"I told you." I said. "I almost died. I was no longer in my body. I saw many things. I saw your father. Your father was wrong, Garrick. He was wrong to say things like that. He was cruel. A father should encourage his son to become better. Yours took pleasure in putting you down. You can be better than he. It is never too late to change. You can refuse to believe the insults. Accept my apology, become a better man than he, be someone your mother would be proud of."

I stood up. Garrick said nothing, but he no longer glared at me. His face was as stone. I could not tell what emotions, if any, he was going through.

I turned around and went to the door. I could almost feel Garrick's gaze following me.

The guard escorted the warren and I back to the locked doors. The warren and I then continued on to the second set of locked doors and on through the room where the first guards were still playing card games and finally through the first set of locked doors we had passed through.

I sighed an inaudible sigh of relief. I was glad it was over. I could still feel Pascal's presence all around me. I felt at peace. I knew I had done the right thing.

Back through the empty, barren corridors we went, to the room where Asur was still sitting, his head still bent in prayer. He looked up as we entered.

I smiled at him to reassure him and he stood up. I thanked the warren and Asur and I left the building.

I closed my eyes and breathed in the outside air deeply and felt the hot sunshine on my face. In that moment, I greatly appreciated my freedom.

I slipped my hand into Asur's and we slowly started walking up the street.

"How does prayer work?" I asked Asur. "How can you ask God for the conversion of another person when God leaves us all free? We are told that prayer is a very strong thing. If prayer is so strong, how can we still be free to resist the prayer of others?"

"I don't know." Asur replied. "Perhaps praying for someone is actually kind of like your soul appealing to the soul of that other person. Perhaps it is, in a way, a silent calling of one soul to another, as well as to God?"

"Does the soul of the other person hear even when the person does not?" I wondered.

"I do not know."

Epilogue

The shrieks of happy children filled my ears as I sat outside in one of the comfortable garden chairs Asur had bought with me especially in mind. The chairs sat in the shade of a pergola that Asur had built with Karl's help.

A year had passed since we had married and moved to the base community we had helped start up in one of the less populated areas south-east of the Bowl, partway up the side of one of the unnamed mountains of the Ma'hra-deh chain, that encircled the City.

I sipped the last of the iced tea that I had prepared for myself earlier and got up to take the empty glass to the kitchen of our newly built, but simple home.

The homes in our community were all built basically the same, with comfort, practicality and esthetics in mind, but simple. There was nothing fancy about them. Some were bigger, to accommodate larger families, some were smaller, to fit childless couples, but they all had the same basic commodities and the same simple but elegant style.

Ours was no longer the only base community in the city. Another one had sprung up a few kilometres to the east. Both were similar in that the people living there lived as a community and contributed to the upkeep of the common living space according to their particular talents. Each consisted of homes built facing inwards towards a commonly shared inner courtyard. It was in this courtyard that children now played while indulgent adults kept an eye on all of them.

Three sides consisted of homes, and the fourth side consisted of a number of offices and workshops or co-ops where people who had a trade could work while keeping an eye out for their children. The fronts of these offices and co-ops were just off of a fairly busy side-street which led directly to the marketplace not too far below.

We were in a good spot for attracting customers, and attract them we did. The women's lace and clothing co-op in particular was doing extremely well. It was quickly becoming well-known for the quality of the lace and the quality of the workmanship put into the clothing.

There was also a furniture co-op that was starting to become well-known and the ceramics workshop would not be long in taking off as well, I thought.

The people that lived here offered each other mutual support as well as pooling resources in order to start up new business. We were also able to more easily help each other out in small ways such as taking turns caring for each other's children.

Respecting each other's privacy and property was important however, so people got out of their business what they put in. And everyone had a small private terrace in the front of their homes. In this way, we hoped to gain the benefits of communism but also the freedom and the right to one's own property and the value of individual work that capitalism offered.

I placed my empty glass in the sink in my kitchen and glanced up at the portrait on the wall.

Erin and I smiled out at me from the portrait. We were both dressed in graduation gowns and were enthusiastically showing off our diplomas in social work. I had graduated from the University of San Isidor and a month later had married Asur. I had been working as a social worker in our little community and in the general vicinity for just under a year now, and enjoyed the contact I had with people immensely. To help people help themselves was an immense joy for me.

Just below that portrait was another one of Maria and Alberto, on their most recent visit to the City to visit us. Alberto stood just behind Maria with his arms around her and his hands clasping hers over her swollen belly.

Maria had given birth to a daughter three months ago, and they had called her Rosa. Asur and I were the very proud godparents of this beautiful little girl.

Asur continued to manage his father's factory and in general the people who worked for him were happy to work there.

Although we both deeply desired children, we did not yet have any, but this morning I had been to see the doctor. As soon as Asur walked in the door this evening, I would tell him the wonderful news. He was going to be a father at last.

I smiled to myself and went to the bathroom to fix my hair and makeup before coming back to the kitchen to fix what had become his favourite meal, seafood paella.

Information about saints was taken from the following websites:

http://en.wikipedia.org/wiki/Pio_of_Pietrelcina
http://en.wikipedia.org/wiki/Joseph_of_Cupertino
http://www.pgdiocese.bc.ca/roseprince/

CPSIA information can be obtained at www.ICGtesting.com
Printed in the USA
LVOW071917221111

256123LV00004B/53/P